THE COLD

RICH HAWKINS

Published by Horrific Tales Publishing 2019

http://www.horrifictales.co.uk

A CIP catalogue record for this book is available from the British Library

ISBN: 978-1-910283-24-0

THE COLD

BY

RICH HAWKINS

"...throw roses into the abyss and say: 'here is my thanks to the monster who didn't succeed in swallowing me alive.'"

- Friedrich Nietzsche

PROLOGUE

Two men found Seth in a crumpled heap on his back, half-buried in a snow drift.

Shivering and confused, each breath a wheezing gasp from sore lungs, he looked up at the men and muttered incoherently. The pain in his bones, in his bruised and impact-softened limbs, muddled his thoughts. Encrusted blood around his left eye, from a shallow gash on his forehead, clouded his vision. His mouth tasted of metal and one of his molars was cracked. He remembered crawling from the wreck of the train to this spot near a blackened and snow-burdened tree. He smelled oil, diesel, and burnt electrics.

"We thought you were dead," said one of the men. He was chubby and pink-cheeked, squinting from one puffy and bruised eye. A Batman t-shirt was visible past the front opening of his thick coat. He grimaced as the wind swept flecks of snow at his face.

"Only half-dead, by the looks of him," said the other man, scratching his beard and frowning. He looked down at Seth. "Anything broken?"

"I don't think so," Seth said.

"Are you all right?" the chubby man asked.

"Looks fucked," the other man said.

"I'm okay, I think," Seth said, wincing at the low ringing in his ears as he sat up. Red bells hammered inside his head. He rubbed his aching jaw. With one hand he scraped the dried blood from around his eye then looked into the middle distance, where the train's three carriages lay on their sides in the field adjacent to the tracks. The train had obliterated several trees and cut large gouges into the snow-covered earth. Shards of shattered glass gleamed on the ground amongst scraps of broken plastic, splintered wood and torn metal. The middle of the front carriage had been ripped open.

Pale fog reduced visibility to less than forty yards in all directions.

And then there were the crumpled bodies around the wreckage of the train, the falling snow slowly softening their outlines.

"Jesus Christ." Seth looked away from the devastation. Tears welled in his eyes as he stared at his trembling hands. A sob caught in his throat.

"Were you with anybody?" one of the men said. Seth was barely listening, but he shook his head, dropping his hands to his lap as he felt the world lurch away from him. His harsh breathing was the only sound as the snow fell against his eyes and his sore face.

The men pulled him up. He stood on watery legs and murmured his gratitude to the two men as they helped him along the ground. They passed the indistinct form of a woman lying mostly sunken in a snowdrift. Her arms were twisted the wrong way and the stiffened fingers of one hand poked from the snow like upturned roots. Before he turned away, stepping over a raggedy, half-frozen teddy bear belly-up on the ground, Seth noticed a wedding ring on her finger.

The men brought him under the bough of a wind-lashed oak. Injured people sat or crouched, huddled in blankets nursing broken limbs, lacerations, concussions. A man sat against a pile of suitcases, bandages wrapped around his head, moaning softly to himself. A woman lay on her back upon a blanket, eyes fluttering, with one side of her face red and exposed. Beside her a young boy, with his left leg gone below the knee - the stump wrapped untidily in gauze and strips of cloth - passed in and out of consciousness, his mouth moving soundlessly.

Several other people milled about or tended to the wounded with meagre supplies from a first aid kit. They paid little attention to Seth. Their faces were slack with shock, their movements meandering and aimless.

"At least you'll be out of the snow," said the bearded man, cringing against a gust of wind and icy flecks.

Seth sat against the base of the trunk and winced as the muscles in his legs twitched and cramped. The cold slowed the blood in his veins, muddied his thoughts, and numbed his limbs.

A young woman with pale blonde hair gave him a coat to use as a blanket. She smiled sadly and, before Seth could thank her, she moved away to check on someone else. He looked out from under the tree and watched the snow fall and bustle. The sky was without definition, waxen and unending.

The bearded man crouched near Seth. "It shouldn't be snowing. It's summer. This shouldn't be happening."

"It came out of nowhere," the chubby man said, sniffling and wiping his nose with the back of his hand. He folded his arms and shifted on his feet, trying to stay warm. "Conditions will only worsen once it gets dark. The temperature will drop."

The bearded man took a small bottle of water from his coat pocket and handed it to Seth. "What's your name?"

"Seth Murphy." He drank several sips then returned the bottle.

"I'm Miles."

"My name's Andy," said the chubby man.

"Thank you for helping me," Seth said. The muscles of his face were slack, as though they'd been loosened by the force of the crash. "I can't thank you enough."

Miles gestured to the other people around them. "We're the only survivors. Fourteen of us."

Seth said nothing. He felt like crying and laughing at the same time, but he was capable of neither.

Miles looked towards the train tracks. "It's been over an hour since the crash. The emergency services should have arrived by now. This place should be teeming with ambulances and police."

"The snow might have blocked the roads and the railway line," Andy said. "We can't even get a phone signal out here, to phone 999. We just need to wait. It must be the weather."

"Of course it's the weather," Miles said. "It's snowing in fucking summer."

Seth fumbled in his pockets and took out his smartphone. He swiped his thumb across the screen, trying to unlock it, but he'd already noticed the cracks and shattered bits of metal and plastic, and knew it was a hopeless and broken thing.

He dropped the phone on the ground and left it there.

"Do you remember what happened?" Miles asked Seth. "Did you see what caused us to crash?"

He tried to recall the bits and pieces drifting in his mind. Little fragments of the time just before the train left the tracks.

"I fell asleep, and when I woke up, I saw the snow outside the windows. People were talking about the snow. Then, I'm not sure what happened. I can't remember." But the memory *was* there. The image flooded his system with adrenaline and anxiety.

He just couldn't bring himself to tell them about the thing he'd glimpsed in the snowstorm, moments before the train crashed.

CHAPTER ONE

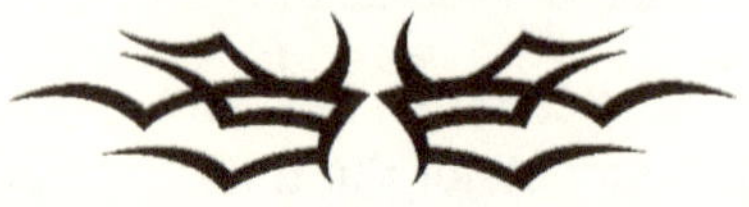

The people on the station platform waited for the train, preoccupying themselves with phones and paperback novels, newspapers and magazines. Those without distractions stared down at their feet or at the tracks below them, lost in their thoughts, while others turned to look down the line, watching for the train to appear. A young couple surrounded by assorted suitcases and bags argued in whispers and stifled movements, careful not to raise their voices and draw glances from the crowd. An old man coughed damply into his hand and wiped it on the front of his coat, then pulled a handkerchief from one pocket and dabbed at the corners of his mouth. Next to him a teenage girl picked at her fingernails, her face set in a frown. The automated voice on the PA system droned a rambling incantation.

Seth stood with his back against a concrete pillar, his arms folded. The temperature was dropping sharply. He stared down the line, urging the train to arrive so he could leave Southampton and the memory of the unsuccessful job interview behind. The air of the city was tainted, clotting in his lungs and tightening his chest. The tall buildings, busy streets, loud music and chattering pedestrians on pavements and in shop doorways had all increased his anxiety and nervous tension as he'd walked to the job interview, and it had been a disaster.

He'd been late, drawing barely-disguised disapproval from the two suited men across the table from him, and once the stammering of his words and the trembling in his hands started, that was the end of that. And now the train back to Somerset was ten minutes late. He checked the time on his phone and breathed through his teeth. The backs of his legs ached with cramps and his eyes stung. He read the text sent by his father just before midday, two hours ago.

Good luck with interview today. Don't be late. Your mother had a bad morning after you left the house. Kept asking for you - she thought you'd run away from home. I explained that it would be a bit weird for our twenty-five year old son to do that. She didn't get the joke. At least she's sleeping now and seems to be okay. Take care, my boy.

Seth put the phone back in his pocket when he heard the distant rumble of the approaching train. He thought about his mother; the Alzheimer's had taken much of her mind in the past year and she was fading a little more with each day. The memories of her before the disease were bittersweet and treasured. It was how she should be remembered, especially once she was gone. Of course his father would be inconsolable when the time came; it would be an effort to bring the old man back from that. It made him question his decision to apply for a job some distance away from home. Just the thought of it all broke Seth's heart and made him nauseous. He swallowed to relieve the thickening of his throat, and blinked away the dampness in his eyes.

The sound of the train grew louder.

The people on the platform turned their heads to look down the track. Reading material was put away. Bags were readied and lifted. Someone laughed nervously. The crowd began clamouring as the train appeared from around the curve of the track. There was no announcement from the speaker system, but nobody cared, because the train was in sight now.

The few dozen people gathered near the edge of the platform as the train scraped and slowed to a stop. Its engine thrummed as it idled. The doors hissed open and several passengers disembarked, leaving the three carriages mostly empty. Seth slouched at the back of the crowd, the skin on the back of his neck prickling from a cold draught that found the openings in his clothes.

He let an old lady step on ahead of him. He minded the gap and moved through the doorway. Behind him a man in a damp-smelling coat kept nudging the backs of his legs with an oversized suitcase.

The stuffy air inside the train irritated his sore throat. Hopefully there was a drinks trolley on board.

He found two seats halfway down the second carriage and sat down, removing his tie and placing it on the seat beside him. He sighed deeply and pinched between his eyes, relieved to be one step closer to home. All he had to do now was sit there until his stop at Yeovil train station, where he'd then get a taxi back home.

Relaxing for the first time all day, he leaned his head back and looked out the window as the last few people boarded. The carriage filled with conversation and dull mutterings, blended with the tinny leaking of music from earphones.

Once everyone was seated, the doors shut and dampened the sound from outside. A whistle shrilled from somewhere. Moments later the train was building up speed along the track, leaving Southampton behind.

"Thank fuck for that," he whispered.

Relieved that no one had sat next to him, he closed his eyes and thought of home.

*

When he saw the snow falling against his window to shroud the world beyond, he thought he must have been asleep and dreaming to see such impossible things.

He raised his head from behind his seat and looked around. The remaining passengers on the carriage watched the snow. With a brief shiver he pulled up the collar of his coat and zipped it up at the front. The train shuddered on the track. Metal rattled somewhere under the carriage. A little girl was crying a few seats behind him.

He strained his eyes to see beyond the snow, but visibility ended only a few yards past the glass. Shapes flitted amidst the descending flakes. There could have been faces out there, staring back at him from the fading daylight. His eyes were playing tricks.

But there *was* something else out there.

And when he glimpsed the colossal shadow-like form of writhing limbs and tendrils lurching towards the train, his eyes stretched wide and his bones seized up as if with a terrible palsy. He tried to call out, to warn the others, but the words stuck in his throat.

The sound of screeching metal filled the inside of the carriage, followed by shrieking inertia and juddering shocks. Covering his head with hands, Seth turned away from the windows as they cracked and shattered, glass shards exploding inwards. The air filled with sharp projectiles. Snow bustled through the broken windows to smother the passengers.

All around him the wind roared, people screamed, and something vast and unknowable responded with cries of its own.

CHAPTER TWO

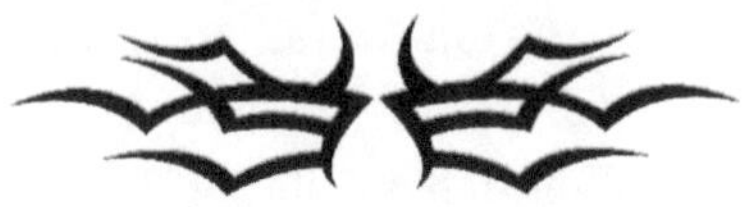

Over an hour had passed since Seth had been pulled from the snow, but so far no emergency services had arrived at the crash site. Miles and Andy volunteered to walk up the tracks to the next train station and find help.

Not wanting to be left behind with the injured and dying, Seth asked to tag along. Miles checked if he was well enough to make the walk, and seemed doubtful but Seth said he'd be fine.

"It might be a long walk," Miles told him.

"No problem."

"You sure?"

"Yeah."

"Can we go now?" said Andy. "Please."

Seth's constant thoughts about the terrible thing he'd seen before the train crash made him nauseated and dismayed. But it was better to do something useful instead of just waiting around to be rescued.

Leaving the other survivors behind, they went off into the snow, shivering in jackets unsuitable for such severe weather. From within his thin hood, Seth stared straight ahead down the tracks as far as possible in the white-out. Hands entrenched in his pockets, he moved with an awkward limp, ignoring the crawling pain in his legs and feet. Thirst irritated his throat. On both sides of the tracks visibility was down to a few yards, now. The air seemed grainy, imbued with diffused light. Silence except for their footfalls and respiration. Not even the sounds of birds or distant traffic. The falling snow suffocated all noise beyond them.

The three men walked to one side of the tracks, trampling through the pristine layer of snow upon the grass, gravel and dirt. Miles moved in front, checking the way ahead between futile attempts to get his phone working. Andy walked abreast of Seth, coughing into his hands. The skin of his face was blotchy.

The falling snow and fog formed a pale shroud of nothingness behind them. Seth suddenly felt that if they stopped walking, the nothingness would catch them, consume them, and obliterate any sign of their presence. Wipe them from the face of the earth.

Andy took a tissue from his pocket and dabbed at his nose. His voice was nasal and quiet. "It feels like we're the only people left in the world."

Seth looked around. "Don't say that. Please don't say that."

"You were thinking the same?"

"A little bit."

"Didn't mean to spook you."

"It's okay."

Miles glanced back at them and frowned.

"Can you believe what happened?" Andy said. "We were in a fucking train crash. That's mental."

"It doesn't feel real."

Andy gave a little laugh that didn't sound right.

Seth thought again of the immense thing of shadow he'd seen before the crash. His breath rattled out of his mouth. His knee joints scraped as he walked.

"Where you from, man?" Andy asked.

"A village called Briar Slope."

"Never heard of it."

"It's near Yeovil."

"Oh yeah, I know Yeovil. Been there a few times. I'm from Bristol."

"I thought so," said Seth.

"Why's that?"

"Your accent."

Andy snorted, wiping his nose. "Can't argue with that. Yours is quite broad, huh?"

"Somerset born-and-bred. The people in Southampton could tell straight away I was a redneck."

"I'm sure it wasn't that bad," said Andy.

"It really was. Never mind, it's the least of my concerns right now. How far until we reach the next station?"

"Not too far, I think," Miles told them.

"I'm fucked," said Andy. "I need a sit down." His face was aggravated and reddened by the cold. Bits of snow had gathered upon the wispy hair on his doughy chin.

"Keep moving," Miles said.

Andy glared at his back and muttered, "Yes, sir," under his breath.

Seth was craving hot sweet tea and painkillers, and thinking of a warm bed, when a flapping sound above made him pause. He looked up, scanning for any movement, but there was nothing but the snow coming down at him. He seemed to be the only one to have heard it. It had sounded too big to be a songbird, so it was probably a buzzard or a large crow.

He pictured large wings of leathery skin and membrane.

"You all right?" Andy asked him.

Seth lowered his face from above and gave a shaky nod. "Thought I heard something."

"Heard what?"

"Nothing, I think. It doesn't matter."

But as they walked on, Seth couldn't help glancing up several times at the pallid sky. There was just the steady snow. That was all. He shook his head and exhaled deeply, the breath trembling out of him and misting in the air.

In the end, he forced himself to stop looking and faced straight ahead, placing one foot in front of the other and praying that the train station would appear soon.

CHAPTER THREE

They reached the train station as the pale sky began to lose its light, and by the time they'd trudged up the gentle slope to the platform they were ready to drop.

Seth hunched over, breathing through clenched teeth, his legs feeling like thin sticks. Andy rested against a pillar and belched wetly. Miles brushed snow from his coat and scanned their surroundings.

They gathered close together, shivering and looking about the two platforms, expecting a staff member to appear. But the platforms were deserted and no one came out to meet them. Bags and suitcases had been left behind, with no sign of their owners. The wind wailed and whispered under eaves and around metal beams, blowing snow under the roofs of the two platforms, where it gathered in dusted scatterings amidst and upon the discarded bags. A metal sign flapped and clanged.

The door to the ticket office had been left ajar by the last person to use it, and now thumped against its frame.

Andy's eyes were watery and forlorn. He buried his hands in his pockets. "Where are all the people?"

No one answered.

*

They found a half-frozen trail of smeared blood running from the centre of the platform all the way to one end where it stopped abruptly, as though whoever was dragged there had simply vanished.

"This can't be happening," Andy repeated several times, before he put his hand over his mouth. He stepped back, shaking his head.

Miles crouched next to where the blood trail ended. He reached out to touch it, but thought better of it at the last moment. He stood and moved away.

The three men looked at each other, then again at the blood, before retreating from the edge of the platform.

Seth thought again of the terrible thing he'd seen before the train crash, and bit down on his tongue to keep silent.

*

While snow pattered against the large windows, the men searched the ticket office and the waiting rooms, but found no sign of life. The heaters inside the main building were cold and the lights didn't work. The ticket machines stood darkened and useless. The landline phones were dead, without even a dial tone.

They found no more blood.

Seth hugged himself for warmth. His insides felt loose. Andy kept shaking his head as he glanced around.

Miles said the power was down because of the weather, but didn't sound convinced by his own speculation, and the expression that Seth glimpsed briefly on his face confirmed it.

*

They searched the rest of the station, but it was completely deserted in the deepening cold, a silent place of thickening shadows and abandoned luggage. Miles found a utility knife in a desk drawer and his eyes met Seth's as he retracted the blade, but neither man said anything.

"Just in case," Miles said. "There might be some bad people hanging around, somewhere..."

Seth didn't reply.

The snow kept falling.

CHAPTER FOUR

Miles led them through the main doors out to the car park, which was empty save for a few scattered vehicles left in their spaces upon the snowy tarmac. The cars were uniform shapes slumping under a thick layer of snow, and the white-out shrouded the edges of the car park and the small town beyond.

The silence was oppressive, full of threats and portent, amplifying the tolling of Seth's pulse inside his head. It was enough to subdue the men. Seth looked down at the red stains in the snow and put one hand to his mouth.

Andy crouched down to carefully pick up a discarded smartphone. He stood again, brushing it clean with the sleeve of his coat, and then he switched it on.

"It still works," he said.

"Let me guess," said Miles. "The network's down."

Andy nodded, his shoulders slumping.

Miles spat. "Fuck's sake."

Andy's forefinger moved upon the phone's screen. He looked at Miles and Seth. "Uh, fellas, there's a video."

"What do you mean?" asked Seth.

Andy was already watching it. His eyes widened. "Holy shit. You should see this."

Seth and Miles stood either side of him as he pressed the 'replay' icon and turned up the volume. The small screen darkened and twitched as the video began to play. The footage was shaky, indistinct, with panicked voices and the sound of a child crying. Then it steadied somewhat to show glimpses of people hurrying through the waiting room inside the station. Seth thought he heard a scream from behind the people, perhaps out on the platform. Then the crowd emerged from the station and stumbled into the car park the three men now stood in. Snow fell heavily. The phone's camera was raised towards the sky as a woman cried out and an immense shadow fell over the group. There was a glimpse of something gargantuan and awful with a nest of glowing white eyes, before the phone fell to the ground to record the screams, flailing feet and spraying blood.

A few seconds later the footage cut out.

"Jesus Christ!" said Miles. "What the hell was that?"

Seth shook his head slowly. He looked around at the shapes of half-frozen blood slowly being erased by the falling snow, and then put a hand against an abandoned car so he wouldn't keel over. The world swayed around him for a moment.

"Was that real?" said Andy. "Was that fucking real?"

Miles gestured to the blood on the ground. "If not, it's a hell of a prank."

"It didn't leave any bodies," Seth muttered.

Andy looked sharply at him. "What are you saying?"

"What do you think he's saying?" snapped Miles.

From out of the distance, beyond the car park and the falling snow, came the deep roaring of something monstrous and huge. It reverberated in the air then faded away, leaving the men in stunned silence. Seth backed up against the car as the breath hitched in his chest. His heart faltered for a moment. Andy dropped the smartphone and stepped back, his throat working, hands at his sides with nothing to do.

Miles didn't move. He stared out into the white veil of snow and vapour.

The roar of the unknown thing was followed by a shrill wailing from a different direction, far away. It didn't sound human, and it pierced the air, seeming to rear and fall into the sky, wavering in the falling snow, before it stopped as abruptly as it had begun.

Seth tried to picture what could make such sounds, but his imagination didn't seem capable. It was enough to bring tears to his eyes. He remembered the massive, writhing shadow he'd seen before the train crash. Such things weren't real. *Couldn't* be real. It was preposterous. It was madness to even be contemplated.

He wrapped his arms around his chest, shivering and sniffling, aching in his bones.

Andy looked at them both, in turn. "We need to get back inside."

Miles stared straight ahead, as if waiting for something to emerge from the nothingness of snow and fog. His hands were clenched into fists, the knuckles white, his brow creasing in wrinkled lines. He looked older than he had a moment ago.

"All right," he said in a hushed voice, his mouth barely moving. "Let's go. It'll be dark soon."

And as they turned to go back inside, other prehistoric

cries and awful shrieks rose from beyond them. It sounded as if all hell and chaos had come to the world.

CHAPTER FIVE

The three men sheltered in the waiting room, terrified and cold and mostly clueless. There was just silence except for the whisper of snow falling to cover the bloodstains in the car park.

None of them spoke for a long while. Seth slumped against a wall and dabbed at his eyes with the heels of his hands. He tried not to panic when he thought of his parents, but he was starting to be overwhelmed by trauma, shock and fear. He felt as though he was losing himself in the aftermath.

Miles stood by one of the windows that looked out upon the car park, keeping watch for whatever dwelt out there in the snow.

Andy sat in the middle of a row of seats in the centre of the room. He let out a low yawn. Bruises darkened the skin underneath his eyes, which were bloodshot and watery. He fidgeted and looked around, his expression vague and soft. He looked like a little boy hoping that everything would get better. Seth could sympathise. Everything had changed and the immediate future seemed hostile and uncertain. Cold dread ached in his gut.

The shadows in the waiting room were darkening and spreading as dusk began to fall.

"Monsters," Andy said. "Fucking hell. That's what we heard out there, yeah? That's what we saw on that video? And all that blood was from people, right? People's blood? Holy fuck."

Miles turned away from the window and slumped into a plastic chair. "I think we're in trouble."

"No shit," said Andy.

"What do we do now?" Seth asked, trying to keep his hands warm in his pockets.

Andy sniffled, wiped his nose, not taking his eyes from the floor. "Good question. What the fuck do we do?"

"I don't know," Miles said.

Andy turned his head towards Seth. "What do you think? Any ideas?"

Seth scratched at his mouth. "Maybe we should just get back to the train."

"I'm not going back out there, mate," said Andy."

"We can't just leave those people at the crash site. They're relying on us to get help."

Andy shook his head and gave a weak shrug. "Maybe there is no help."

"What do you mean?"

"What do you *think* I mean?"

"Andy's right," said Miles. "We should assume that no one is coming to help us or the other survivors." He let out a breath that seemed to deflate parts of him.

"So, what do we do?" Seth replied. "Just wait here and see what happens?"

"I don't know."

Andy wore an expression of dismay. "I'm not going back

out there. Fuck all that."

"We have to, eventually," Miles told him.

"Not after what we've seen and heard today. No way."I'd rather piss glass, mate."

Seth wiped his stinging eyes and gave a sour laugh of desperation and bewilderment. "This is a nightmare."

Miles rose from his chair. "I'm going to head back to the train."

Andy looked up at him. "Did you not see that video?"

"We can't leave them stranded. We can't abandon them. Something has to be done."

"You'll die if you go back out there." Andy's voice was low and forlorn. "You'll die for nothing."

"I've made my decision," said Miles. He buttoned the front of his coat. Then he pulled up his hood and fetched the first aid kit from the ticket office. "You're both welcome to come with me, of course."

Seth just shook his head weakly. His legs felt heavy and useless. He lowered his head, unable to meet Miles' gaze. Shame warmed his face and burned in his throat and chest.

"Don't go out there," Andy muttered. "You won't come back."

Miles held the first aid kit under one arm and walked to the doors that led to the platform outside. He paused, looked back at Seth and Andy, and told them to take care.

But when he opened the door, he was confronted by a woman standing on the other side of the threshold. He stepped back quickly and flecks of snow followed him.

Seth and Andy rose and stared at the woman. The wind rose to a torturous keening, shaking the walls and the roof.

The woman was trembling, covered in dried splatters of blood. Seth recognised her from the crash site; she'd been the one trying to take care of the injured. Her mouth was wide open, gawping, and then she drew in a shivering breath and screamed until her legs gave out beneath her and she collapsed in the doorway.

CHAPTER SIX

"What happened, Ruby?" Miles asked her.

"All the others are dead," she muttered, hunched over in her seat and rocking slightly. She couldn't hold eye contact with anyone for more than a moment. The forefinger and thumb of her left hand fiddled with the small silver cross hanging from a necklace chain around her neck. Seth had cleaned her face with wet wipes from a packet he'd found in one of the abandoned holdalls on the platform. He sat beside her, but was afraid to offer anything more than comforting words.

Miles fetched a jacket from the ticket office and draped it over her juddering shoulders. She pulled the jacket around herself and then took a deep pull from the bottle of water Andy had given her. She wiped her mouth and looked at Miles, then Seth, and finally at Andy, who stood across from her in horrified silence.

"They came out of the sky," Ruby said.

"What did?" replied Miles.

She hesitated. "Flying creatures with black wings and red eyes. Had to be half-a-dozen of them. Horribly thin and tall, shaped like an overgrown insects." She put her hand over her mouth, muffling her words as tears filled her eyes. "Oh God. All the people died. They're all gone. Jesus help me."

"How did you escape?" Miles barely disguised the tremor within his voice.

Ruby shivered then let out a deep sob. "I hid in one of the train carriages - in a stinking toilet compartment - while the creatures fed. Once they were gone, I made a run for it, hoping to find you three."

"At least someone made it out," Andy said, before looking away and bowing his head.

"It's OK," Seth told Ruby, and placed a comforting hand on her upper arm.

"So, what do we do now?" Andy asked, slumping onto a chair. "Do we have a plan?"

"Considering what's happened, maybe we should stay here tonight," said Miles. "No point in returning to the crash site, and at least we can shelter here until morning. Any objections?"

There were none. Seth didn't have the energy to walk to the next room, let alone the nearest town or village. He thought about his parents, and had to close his eyes against the pang of guilt.

"We need to secure this room as best we can," Miles said. "I'll look for some food and water while Seth and Andy barricade the doors. We might get visitors during the night."

"Do you think a load of furniture will stop anything?" Andy asked bitterly.

"Probably not. Do you have a better plan?"

He shrugged. "No."

"Then get it done. No time to waste."

*

Seth and Andy pushed a low table against the door that led to the car park then piled it with chairs. At least if anything did try to gain entry during the night, the noise of it would wake them, he reflected.

The falling snow had lessened slightly, but it was impossible to see anything out in the darkness beyond the windows.

Miles had found a torch, which now served as their only source of light besides Andy's cigarette lighter. He'd also recovered a crowbar and some musty blankets from the store room, and two chocolate bars from a rucksack in the ticket office. They shared the chocolate then settled down for the night. Ruby had passed out, lying across three seats with a blanket placed over her. She muttered in her sleep, her face wan, eyelids fluttering as she dreamed.

Seth, Miles and Andy sat beside each other on the floor with their backs against the wall, watching the door and the windows. They'd closed the curtains, but Miles kept the torchlight directed at the floor, just in case something was stalking in the night.

Andy offered Miles and Seth each a cigarette. Miles refused, but Seth took one after a moment's hesitation. Andy lit it for him, and he pulled smoke into his lungs. The inside of his head swayed a little as he exhaled through his mouth with an exhausted sigh. He hadn't smoked since his teenage years, and he coughed heavily into his hand. It soothed his anxiety though, and slowed the blood through his veins for a moment.

"Where did you find them?" Seth asked.

"Someone left them on the edge of a sink in the men's toilets."

"Oh, I see."

"A lucky find."

"Yeah, lucky us."

"We can't stay here," Miles said. He sipped a small mouthful of water. The taps in the bathrooms had offered only drops.

Andy took a drag on his cigarette. "Couldn't we wait here, in case the police arrive?"

Miles shook his head, staring at the crowbar in his hands. "I don't think the police are coming, Andy."

"You can't be sure of that."

"Look outside," Miles said. "No one is going to save us. What if the snow and the creatures aren't just a local phenomenon? What if it's affected a greater area?"

"You think the snow and the monsters are linked?" asked Seth. He felt stupid for not making the connection earlier.

Andy tapped the tip of his cigarette into the old mug he was using as an ashtray. "How is that possible?"

Miles looked at him. "None of this should be possible. And yet here we are."

"What the fuck caused it? A friend of mine is a bit of a conspiracy theorist. I remember him saying stuff about governments experimenting with weather control satellites. I thought it was bollocks at the time, but now..."

"I don't know," said Miles, wrinkling his nose.

Andy continued. "Maybe the Large Hadron Collider caused it. Fucking around with particles and all that stuff, opening up wormholes and god-knows-what. Maybe they fucked something up really badly."

"From Switzerland?" Miles asked.

They each pondered the possibilities of scale for a moment, shaken by the thought of a global phenomenon. Seth tried to bring it back to a more manageable level.

"Do you think the whole country is affected?"

"We can't say for sure," Miles said. "That's why we have to leave tomorrow - in case this is all confined to a small area."

Andy finished his cigarette and dropped it into the mug. "What if there's some sort of quarantine?"

"I don't know," Miles said. "We're cut off. We don't know anything about what's happening." He let out a ragged breath and rested the back of his head against the wall. "It's probably best not to speculate until we know more about our situation. We should get some sleep, and then leave in the morning. It'll be safer than travelling in the dark."

"I won't be able to sleep tonight," said Andy.

"You should try."

"I'm fucking exhausted," Seth said.

Andy snorted. "Proper shit day. Worst day ever."

"Get some rest, fellas," Miles told them. "You'll be glad of it tomorrow."

Andy gave a small, sour laugh. "Let's just hope the monsters don't eat us in our sleep."

CHAPTER SEVEN

Seth dreamed of returning home to find everything covered in snow. Crows perched atop the roof of his parents' house. Upon the snow, where the lawn should have been, were yellowed bones picked clean of their meat. And in the distance, black tendrils writhing and coiling, the immense form of a god-monster wailed to the sky and ruin of the wasteland.

*

They readied themselves in the first light of morning. Ruby sat nearby, eating a piece of chocolate Miles had saved for her, watching the men dismantle the barricade. Andy smoked one of his last cigarettes while he peered from a window and looked outside.

"See anything?" Seth asked him.

"Snow."

"Yeah."

"You OK?"

"I think so."

Miles handed Seth the utility knife. "It's not much, but it'll be better than nothing when we're out there."

Seth used his thumb to slide out the small retractable blade, which was slightly rusted but still sharp enough to be useful. "Thanks."

Miles hefted his crowbar. "No worries."

Andy stepped towards them, the dwindling cigarette in his hand. "Don't I get a weapon?"

"If you can find something."

"Yeah, I'll find a broom handle or maybe a plastic fork…"

Miles ignored him and looked at Ruby, who was just staring at the floor. "We ready to go?"

Seth shifted on his feet and took slow breaths. "Not really."

"Same here," said Andy. "This is a bad idea."

"Let's just go," Ruby told them. "There has to be help somewhere."

*

They stepped outside, staying close together, the snow falling in silence around them. The white fog and snowfall brought visibility down to less than five metres all around. Their breath misted in the air. Wrapped in their coats and a few scavenged blankets, they glanced about, watching for movement in the car park as Miles led them on with his crowbar in both hands.

They kicked through a thick layer of snow.

"This is mental," Andy said. "I can't believe we're doing this."

"How far?" Ruby asked. Seth was helping her along.

Miles pointed ahead. "Once we're out on the street, we need to keep going straight through the nearby park, and then the police station is after that. It's not even a mile away, if I remember correctly."

Their footfalls in the snow sounded clumsy and too loud in the absence of other noises. The shapes of buildings began to coalesce from the white fog and soon the group had made it through the car park and out into the street. When Seth looked over his shoulder, the train station had already faded into the falling snow. It was all he could do not to let out a pained whimper at being out in the open, vulnerable to creatures with sharp teeth and deep hunger.

The group stood in the street, ankle-deep in the layer of snow, huddled like prey animals. The cold air gnawed at the exposed skin of Seth's face and made his teeth chatter. He looked around. No animals or birds, and no sign of people. Parked cars lined one side of the street, and the group had to walk around a Toyota Yaris lying upon its side as they crossed the road. Much of the vehicle had been smashed and dented. He noted shattered windows. Dried blood inside the car.

"No bodies left," said Ruby. "Because they were eaten."

They clambered over the short fence that separated the street from the park and struggled along with aches and worried minds. The gnarled limbs of black trees were laden with snow.

"Keep moving," said Miles. "The police station isn't far away."

"Stop," Andy said.

Miles looked back. "What?"

Andy's voice quietened. "Everyone fucking stop, please."

They halted.

"What is it?" asked Seth. He pulled his hood tighter over his head.

Andy pointed away to their right, where the large, ragged black shape of something on four legs emerged from the white fog, wheezing and baying. It must have been seven feet tall at the shoulder.

"Look at that bastard," he said.

The creature was some kind of boar-like thing, standing on double-jointed limbs. It was a mangy, diseased beast. A row of spines ran down the centre of its back. Pallid udders hung from its underside.

"My God," said Miles.

It opened its tusk-lined mouth and released a near-tortured wailing that reverberated through the air.

They all dropped to a crouch as the creature stamped its hooves upon the ground, kicking up snow. It shook its head from side to side then raised its face to the obscured sky and let out another wail before it vanished into the white fog.

Moments later some other creature screeched in the distance.

Miles led them on again, through the park, and nothing else emerged to slow them down.

CHAPTER EIGHT

Through another silent street, one with several houses smashed to ruin. Damaged sections of walls or ceilings missing. Broken rooms within and glimpses of desolation. Scattered brickwork and toppled chimneys. Shards of glass gleaming in the snow.

"Fucking hell," Andy said, with awe and barely restrained terror. His face appeared slack and gaping.

Ruby looked at Miles. "I thought you said the police station was nearby. Where is it?"

"It's close," Miles muttered.

"How close?" Ruby frowned. Her eyes were damp. "Are we lost?"

"No."

"Are you sure about that?" asked Andy.

A street light lay across the road, bent and twisted at its base by the work of something immensely powerful. A telephone pole leaned crookedly, as if it'd been glanced by a truck or SUV. *Or something else.* Its wires hung slack and bowed.

"Just keep moving," Miles whispered, turning his head to watch their flanks. "Don't stop."

Abandoned snow-covered cars hindered them as they walked along the road towards the police station, and Seth found himself looking inside each one as he passed, through open doors and smashed windows. He thought about all the people who'd lived here and what might have happened to them. He wondered if anyone was hiding in the town, in their houses or amongst the ruins of buildings, hoping for rescue or just trying to survive.

"Maybe everyone was evacuated," he said.

Miles watched the road ahead. "Maybe."

"They're probably all dead," muttered Ruby. She looked at the ground, shaking her head, and said nothing more.

*

They stood facing the police station, shivering in the cold. The front of the building was undamaged, its roof and windowsills covered in snow. The windows were intact. The front doors were closed.

"Do you really think anyone's in there?" Andy asked. He was hunched and cowed.

Miles looked around. "Maybe some survivors are gathered here. It would make sense."

"Nothing makes sense any more," Ruby said. She wiped her mouth. Her eyelids drooped. "I need to sit down."

It took both Miles and Andy to pull open the doors, due to the drifts of snow gathered at the front of the building. They went inside. The reception area was deserted, but untouched by violence, and in the cold morning light it was like a memory of an unchanged world.

No one manned the counter that ran between opposite walls. There was a row of blue plastic seats on metal legs. A wall-rack of leaflets about crime and punishment, human rights, and tips on home security. A fake, smiling family gazed down at the group from a Neighbourhood Watch poster. Smears of dirt on the floor and the smell of old sweat.

The door to the office area beyond the reception was hanging from its hinges.

"Imagine the creature that could do such a thing," Ruby said.

"We have to check inside," Miles said. "There could still be police somewhere here."

"It's a bad idea," said Andy.

Miles glared at him. "Do you have a better one?"

Andy looked away, gave a slight shrug.

They followed Miles as he raised the hinged section of the counter and stepped through the wrecked doorway. He switched on his torch, directed it about the office area and over the shadows on the plush carpet. Nothing moved. No one waited for them at the few desks, where dead monitors sat among the personal effects of the people who'd worked there. Office chairs had been scattered. A filing cabinet lay on its side. The torch beam swept over framed photos and certificates on the walls.

Andy flicked a light switch, but all remained dim and in half-shadows.

"Everyone's gone."

"We have to keep searching," said Miles. "Andy, you wait here with Ruby, while Seth and I check the other rooms."

Andy and Ruby sat down in the nearest chairs. Seth gave Andy the knife.

"Just in case something happens," Seth told him.

"Hurry up," Miles said.

Seth went with him, leaving Andy and Ruby behind, and stalked into the silent corridors that led into the building.

CHAPTER NINE

Seth and Miles found the mutilated corpse of a police officer sprawled on the floor in the interview room. A chair was lying on its side. Blood stained the walls and the floor in spatters.

They stood over the body. The man's hands were missing and part of his face had been torn away to reveal a fixed, bloody grin. His eyes were gone. Deep lacerations punctured his chest and stomach.

Seth put his hand to his mouth. The stench of exposed intestines, mostly chewed and torn, was enough to make him step back to the doorway. Miles didn't move; he appeared almost fascinated.

"He's been partially eaten," Miles said.

"Yeah, looks like it. Do you think whatever did it is still in here somewhere?"

"You should have kept the knife, Seth."

*

More broken and torn bodies littered the corridors farther on. The police officers had been slaughtered. Some of the bodies were missing their heads. Seth had to look away.

"What the fuck did this?" he said, as they both moved slowly towards the holding cells.

Miles kept the torchlight directed straight ahead.

They reached the block of five cells at the back of the building. Each cell door was open. They checked each small room in turn but found nothing. Seth was quietly relieved.

They were heading down the corridor to the locker rooms when Miles halted and put his hand out to stop Seth. They'd passed several pools of drying blood on the floor.

"What's wrong?" Seth asked.

Miles stared down the corridor. He dropped his hand from Seth's shoulder. "Do you hear that?"

"Hear what?"

"Something panting. Like an animal. Something big. Listen."

Seth listened. At first he heard nothing, but then the sound of low grunting and huffing rose from beyond the turn of the corridor.

"It's getting closer," said Miles. The light of his torch reached only several metres before succumbing to the dark.

Seth wiped at his face and looked at Miles. The nausea he'd felt all morning was rising in his chest. "Let's get back to Andy and Ruby. They'll be wondering where we are."

Miles was still staring down the corridor, and when the sounds of movement grew nearer and louder, his face tightened. Seth didn't want to look down the corridor, and in the end he wished he hadn't.

"Holy fuck," he said.

Caught in the torchlight, the creature - a tall, ape-like thing with a pot belly and spindly limbs - reared on its back legs and bellowed at the men as it pounded its chest like a gorilla. A crimson crest, pulsing wetly, topped its wide, solid head and reached almost to the ceiling. Its yawning, bloodstained mouth, crammed with shard-like teeth, was large enough to encompass a child's head. Patchy grey fur over a creased hide of pale skin, all dry and scabbed. Thick hands capable of splintering bone. It was like some terrible subspecies of great ape, a mingling of breeds that had created something abominable. Something not meant to exist in this world.

Seth and Miles winced as it roared inside the cramped corridor space. They backed away, slowly, while the ape-thing stared at them, snorting and wheezing.

Then the two men turned and ran.

*

The creature was quicker, and before they reached the door at the end of the corridor, it was upon them. One second, Miles was running beside Seth, then he was gone. Seth looked back and saw the ape-thing lift Miles from his feet with one great hand and squeeze the man's neck until his eyes bulged and his mouth gaped in agony. He dropped his torch, and when it hit the floor it threw jagged shadows of beast and man together.

Seth slipped in a puddle of drying blood and fell to his knees. He looked back again, legs weak, vision swaying.

After the crowbar was batted out of his grasp, Miles pawed at the creature, but his attempts were useless, and the creature bit off his left hand when it drifted near its mouth. Blood streamed from the stump of Miles' wrist, and he screamed, but only for a few moments before the ape ripped his head from his shoulders.

CHAPTER TEN

Ruby and Andy were already on their feet when Seth staggered into the office. Andy's face was all confusion and fear as he held onto her.

"Move!" Seth said, pulling them both along.

Andy looked over his shoulder and let out a cry. The terrible ape burst through the far doorway, dragging Miles' broken remains in one hand. They blundered through the reception area and stumbled outside.

The snow whirled all about them. Strange, terrifying noises drifting within in the wailing wind. Seth kept them moving, kicking through the drifts of snow along the road.

Something else roared from a nearby street. Seth turned his head towards the sound and caught a glimpse of a shadowy, insectoid shape more than twenty feet tall loping behind cottages and bungalows. Then it was gone and there was just the falling snow.

Andy was struggling to pull Ruby with him. "We're gonna die out here! I won't want to die out here, Seth!"

"Keep moving," Seth shouted. He looked back up the road to see the ape-thing shambling after them on all fours, bellowing and snarling as it went. He led Andy and Ruby through a passageway between two houses and across snow-shrouded ground that was once lawns and neat gardens, then out into the adjacent street to weave between abandoned vehicles.

They stumbled straight into the path of a towering,

tumorous beast of quivering tentacles rising from around a dilating, slopping maw. Its lumpen, slavering mass scuttled on crooked legs that scraped through snow drifts and pushed aside derelict cars as it sensed new prey and turned towards them.

They were rendered speechless by the sight of the monster, which possessed nothing that looked like eyes. It was a blind thing. But with the slavering and shuddering from inside its mouth, the creature seemed to be drawing in their scent, and it broke into a skittering gallop, its tendrils and damp limbs thrashing upon the ground, spraying snow into the air. Its giant mouth convulsed and undulated, and it uttered a piercing wail that filled the street.

Seth stumbled away from a swiping tendril, losing his grip on Ruby, and ran through the charred ruins of a house. He tripped and flailed, somehow keeping his footing, and when he glanced around for the others, they were nowhere to be seen. The snow spat against his face, into his eyes, half-blinding him until he wiped them clean. He gritted his teeth, slogging through the snowfall and lungs straining with each breath, he let out a sob. He was alone and not long for the world.

He collided with Andy as the man stumbled out from a partially-collapsed doorway. Sudden tangle of limbs as they flinched and slipped. They cried out, first in terror and surprise, then in relief, almost falling down together.

Andy's face was flecked with snow and taut with fear, his eyes loose and manic in their bone sockets. He gripped Seth's shoulders and sobbed. Seth imagined that his own face appeared much the same to Andy.

"Where's Ruby?" Seth said.

Andy's mouth wouldn't keep still. "I lost her. I couldn't find her."

Seth looked him. "We'll find her. Come on."

In the flailing snow and wind, they doubled back, watching for the beast or the creature that had killed Miles. Every movement around them was a threat with sharp teeth. Shrill, inhuman cries rose from somewhere in the town.

They halted in the middle of the street. Ahead of them, twenty yards away, Ruby kneeled in the snow, looking down at the silver cross she held between two fingers. Her face was streaked with tears. Then she placed her hands together in prayer and looked up to the low sky.

The blind monster shrieked from nearby.

Andy staggered over to Ruby and pulled her away from the approaching shape of the monster. Seth moved with them as they fled down the street and along slippery pathways until they slowed to an exhausted stagger through the thick drifts. The swirling flecks of snow harried them until they were hunched over and barely walking in the blizzard.

"I think it's lost track of us," Seth said. "What the fuck was it?"

"What was that thing in the police station?" Andy asked, panting and coughing.

"I don't know."

"Poor Miles. Poor bastard."

"It ripped his fucking head off." Seth let out a strangled sob, and his legs lost all their strength. He fell to his knees, exhausted and despondent. Terrified of the world. Andy and Ruby stood over him, their heads bowed against the storm. Ruby's hands were still clasped together, the silver cross dangling from between.

Seth joined her in prayer, and begged to God for salvation. It was all he could do.

CHAPTER ELEVEN

They found an abandoned house on an empty street in the wild wind and snow. There was no sign of monsters, but the daylight was already dimming. Something that sounded like thunder boomed far away and reverberated throughout the sky.

It was like the darkest winter of nightmares. Seth found it difficult to think straight; everything inside his head seemed vague and drifting.

Seth, Ruby and Andy slumped on the sofa in the living room. They had checked the house for occupants both human and otherwise, and found nothing. Like the other buildings in the town, there was no electricity or running water. The walls and floors radiated cold.

Judging by the framed photos, the house belonged to a middle-aged married couple without children. Seth wondered what had become of them, and then decided he didn't want to think any more about it.

Ruby exhaled, rubbed her eyes, and then looked at the floor. She was shivering. "I feel better now. But I don't remember much of what's happened."

Andy leaned forward, holding his face in his hands. "We're the only survivors from the train," said Andy.

"Just us?"

"Yeah."

"Are you okay?" Andy asked her.

She nodded, wiped her mouth. "Yeah. I just need to sit down for a bit."

"Same here."

"Yeah."

Seth stared at the window on the far side of the room; the world beyond was all mist and snow, seemingly empty of life. Dead silence. A sudden image of his parents, hiding from the monsters, flashed through his mind. A wave of hopelessness left him trembling and forlorn. The edges of his vision dimmed. His heart felt slow and heavy. Lactic acid ached in his limbs.

"What shall we do?" asked Andy.

Seth sighed, pushed the memories of Miles' death from his mind. "Stay here for a while. It's not safe outside. Too many people have already died."

They remained on the sofa, in silence, huddled together for warmth.

*

Seth was woken by a tall, hooded figure in a snow-flecked coat, its eyes obscured by snow goggles as it regarded the three of them on the sofa.

Seth blinked, took a sharp intake of breath, as he noticed the rifle in the figure's arms. He'd never seen a gun before in real life, not a proper gun, and the sight of the barrel pointed in his direction turned his guts to water.

"I thought I was alone out here," the intruder said, its voice muffled by the scarf wrapped around the lower half of its face. "Wake up your friends."

*

The man dropped his rucksack on the floor then sat down in an armchair. He stood his rifle against the nearest wall and took off his snow goggles. Then he removed his scarf, pulled back his hood, slumped back and sighed deeply. His haggard face was darkened by black stubble. Seth, Ruby and Andy watched him.

"I was trying to reach the police station," the man said, "but I got turned around in the snowfall. Then I saw your trail in the snow. and thought it best to find the nearest house instead. You left the back door unlocked, by the way. Who are you?"

Painfully aware of the rifle within the man's reach, they spoke their names.

The man nodded. "I'm Bill Weir. Everyone calls me Weir. Christ, I thought I was alone out here."

"We just came from the police station," Andy said.

"How was it?" Weir asked him. "Anyone there?"

"The police are gone," said Seth. He didn't mention the ravaged corpses of the police officers or Miles' death.

Weir rubbed at his face with the heels of his hands. "I didn't expect any different, to be honest." He noticed them staring at him. "Why are you looking at me like that?"

"You're the first person we've seen since the snow began to fall," said Seth.

Weir frowned. "Really?"

Ruby fidgeted with her hands on her lap. "We were on a train. It crashed. We're the only survivors."

"You've had contact with the monsters?"

Seth nodded. "You could say that."

Ruby suppressed a sob.

"Do you know much about what's happened?" said Andy. "Do you know what's going on? You must know something..."

"Please," Ruby muttered.

Weir glanced at each of them. "You've done well to survive without a firearm."

"We've been lucky," Seth said. "Where did you find a gun?"

Weir brushed bits of snow from his coat, before he unzipped it down to his stomach, revealing a tactical vest and a police badge on the left side of his chest. "I'm an Authorised Firearms Officer. One of the few left, I'll bet."

"Is it that bad out there?" Andy asked.

"It's worse than you could ever imagine," said Weir.

Andy snorted. "What's that supposed to mean?" said Ruby.

"It means that normal service will not be resumed."

Seth leaned forward. "What do you know?"

Weir retrieved three small bottles of water from his rucksack and tossed one each to Seth, Ruby and Andy. They unscrewed the caps and drank greedily. Seth had never been so grateful for a drink of bland water. Beside him, Ruby burped into her hand and replaced the cap on the bottle. Andy downed almost his entire bottle in one go.

"Food?" Weir asked them, and when they nodded he threw them a large packet of cheese crackers to share.

They tore into the packet, and Seth had eaten half a dozen crackers before he realised that Weir was watching them. He wiped his mouth and let Andy and Ruby eat the rest. Weir offered a sympathetic half-smile.

"What do you know?" Seth asked him again. "What the fuck has happened?"

Weir looked out the wide living room window at the blizzard. "I'll go back to the beginning, when the snow started to fall, before it all fell apart."

*

Weir spoke in a low voice.

"It was chaos. There were monsters - things that shouldn't have been possible. Horrific things. We were deployed near Salisbury cathedral and within minutes we were overwhelmed. All my colleagues were killed. I think I saw people get *taken* by the snow, but I'm not sure. I remember just firing my weapon at the creatures, and somehow I managed to evade them and survive. I escaped the city. My house was a few miles outside Salisbury, but when I returned there, my wife—" He looked at the floor, wringing his hands, shaking his head as his eyes welled up. "She was dead. Something had...eaten parts of her. Our house had been half-crushed. Most of the village was devastated by something colossal that had passed through. I buried my wife in the back garden and then headed west, searching for any other police units, or the Army maybe. On the way here I saw a monster the size of a fucking mountain."

"What about the rest of the country?" said Seth. "Did you hear anything?"

"The last I heard, it was all over. It's everywhere."

Andy rubbed one side of his face. "What about the rest of the world?"

Weir shrugged. "I don't know. I haven't heard about anything beyond the UK. I'm just heading west trying to find other survivors, and any remains of local government. There has to be something. Have you seen any police or military?"

"None at all," said Seth.

"It all happened so quickly," Weir said. "We didn't stand a chance."

After that, no one said anything for a long while.

CHAPTER TWELVE

As the day dimmed outside, they secured the ground floor of the house and drew the curtains across the windows. On the kitchen table were plates of mouldering food with scattered forks and knives.

A family had lived here, and Seth tried not to think about them, or to to to look at their photos dotted around the rooms.

The four survivors settled in the living room, wrapped in blankets they'd recovered from the linen closet upstairs. It felt safer than being in separate rooms, despite the lure of warm, comfortable beds. Andy had found a packet of cigarettes in a kitchen drawer, and he could scarcely contain his relief. He held the packet close to his chest. Ruby sat beside him, occasionally glancing his way. The silver cross never left her hands.

Weir switched on an LED lantern, and the comforting light painted the lower parts of the walls. He handed a torch to Seth, for use in an emergency. Then he showed them how to check their feet for frostbite; they were relieved to find none. Afterwards, they ate cold food pilfered from the kitchen - baked beans, tinned hot dogs, crisps, and chocolate. After the last two days, it was the best food Seth had ever tasted.

"Where're you headed?" Weir asked them.

"I'm trying to get back to my parents' house," said Seth.

"Where's that?"

"About fifteen miles west of here."

"What about you, Andy?"

Andy swallowed the last of a chocolate bar and wiped his mouth. "I have no idea. Haven't got any family. I live alone in a flat in Bristol. Maybe I'll just stick with you guys."

Ruby glanced at Andy. "I'm from Bristol too. I broke up with my boyfriend a few months ago, and he moved out, so now I rent a shitty little terraced house. There's nothing left there for me."

"Fair enough," said Weir. "Looks like we're all heading west, then. Makes sense to stick together."

Seth stared at the floor. "But I don't know what to do once I get back to my village. I don't even know if my village is still there, let alone my house. What if it's all been destroyed by the monsters? What if my parents are dead? What will I do then? Just wander the country looking for help? I don't know what to do." Sudden panic fluttered in his chest and turned his face hot. He chewed on the inside of his cheek; it was a habit from childhood, one which hadn't done in years. He blinked to clear his misty vision. His hands were shaking.

Andy patted him on the shoulder, but said nothing.

"We'll figure out something," Weir said.

*

Later in the night, while Weir was cleaning his pistol in the light of the lantern, distant shrieks and roaring came from somewhere beyond the town. They all froze and listened to the trampling of a large creature in a nearby street, grinding within the earth, until it faded away and they relaxed again.

Ruby sobbed and bowed her head. Seth closed his eyes, to shut the world out for a few moments, but it didn't work.

"Monsters," Andy said. "Monsters everywhere."

*

During the night, Seth woke from bad dreams to find Andy sitting up and staring at the living room window. In the darkness, the man was little more than a shadow.

Seth cleared his throat, coughed. "You okay?"

"Can't sleep. I'm fucking terrified, man. I don't think I can keep going like this. People like me aren't supposed to..."

"People like you?"

"Weak people."

"You're not weak, Andy."

"We're all weak compared to the monsters."

"We'll be okay." Seth didn't know what else to say. It sounded pathetic, a cruel lie told to a troubled child. "*You'll* be okay."

Andy turned towards him. "Miles is dead. All the people from the train are dead. For fuck's sake, there were babies on that train, Seth. All dead. Jesus Christ."

"I know," he said. "I know."

"None of us are gonna be okay, man. It's all gone."

*

Seth woke again in the darkness some time later and

heard Ruby muttering a prayer beside Andy, who was asleep, on the sofa. Her tender voice, edged with grief, brought tears to Seth's eyes.

He did not interrupt her, even as her prayers became muffled sobs. He tried to go back to sleep, but old memories of his childhood kept him awake into the early hours.

CHAPTER THIRTEEN

In the morning they ate a quick breakfast before heading west out along the main road towards the next town. Seth, Ruby and Andy had swapped their tattered and stained coats for thicker ones from the house. They had replaced their dirty socks and wore three on each foot to keep away the cold. Weir had found suitable boots and gloves for them to wear.

They had also filled a rucksack and a holdall with food, bottled water, and two bottles of cheap vodka Seth had liberated from the back of a cabinet in the living room. Each of the survivors had taken a swig before leaving the house.

Both sides of the dual carriageway were littered with crashed and wrecked vehicles, and Seth didn't look long at the shapes of bodies under the snow before turning away. He held a long-handled axe in one hand; another useful item recovered from the house. The rucksack was slung over his back.

Andy adjusted the holdall across his shoulders and stayed close to Ruby. A carving knife was tucked into his belt. They muttered to each other. Ruby managed a wan smile that barely manifested on her face.

Weir kept watch, scanning around them, cradling his rifle across his chest. He kept the barrel aimed at the ground.

The hardening layer of snow crunched under their boots. The snow was falling lightly, barely at all now, but the white fog obscured visibility all around them.

Whale-like calls and a high-pitched yipping rose from the distance in all directions.

"Mega-fauna," Weir said.

"What?" Seth asked him.

"Big fucking animals," Andy said, before Weir could answer.

Weir snorted, watched the road ahead. "That's right."

Big fucking monsters, Seth thought.

They kept moving.

Seth looked out to the east, across to where the fields of snow disappeared into the fog. Trees were whispering things in the wind. There was no horizon. "Where do you think the creatures are from?"

"They don't belong to this world," Weir said, looking around with his rifle half-raised.

"You reckon they're aliens?" Andy blinked flecks of snow from his eyes.

"They are demons," Ruby said, wiping her face.

Weir shrugged. "They came with the snow. And this is no ordinary snowfall, not in summer."

Seth glanced at the sky. "Summer is dead and gone."

"Do you think the snow will ever stop?" Andy asked.

No one answered.

They walked onwards.

*

It took another hour to reach the outskirts of the next town. They stood on the slope between rows of silent buildings and regarded the devastation and abandonment before them. Several cars were wrecked and crashed at the sides of the road, and inside one was a dead man slumped behind the steering wheel. Two plumes of smoke were rising from separate locations near the centre of town.

Seth looked for shoe prints in the snow, but found none.

Andy's dull eyes flitted about. "More of the same, huh?"

"There must be some people here," said Weir. He was watching the way ahead, his rifle raised. He stood fully upright against the snow and wind. With one hand he wiped his goggles clean.

The sound of distant roaring and thudding rose again, and rang out for over a minute, before fading away. Ruby shivered.

"That sounded like a fight between two giants! Closer than before," said Andy.

They went on, past industrial buildings, desolate car parks and looted shops. Snow crackled and groaned under them. Voices in the wind. A line of terraced houses had been reduced to snow-covered rubble and debris.

Seth's bones ached. His joints scraped in dry sockets when he moved his limbs. It felt as though he hadn't slept in days, yet he remembered terrible dreams about monsters and loneliness. He swept his gaze around the forlorn places about them and saw no one aside from mutilated bodies being slowly consumed by snow drifts. Dead faces stared out at him.

Weir halted, and raised his rifle while the others stopped either side of him. They followed his aim down the road. Andy made a low sound and stepped back. Ruby held onto his arm.

The wolves appeared from out of a ruined house and were crossing the street towards a stretch of open ground. Suddenly they stopped in the road and turned towards the survivors. There were seven of them, led by a haggard alpha, motionless as they appraised the new arrivals to the town. Their fur was flecked with snowflakes.

Andy whispered, "Do you think they're just passing through, like us?"

"Be quiet." Weir spoke without looking at him, and kept the rifle raised.

"Must have escaped from a zoo or a safari park. Longleat, maybe? Would you be able to shoot them all before they reached us?"

"I told you to be quiet, Andy," Weir hissed.

"Sorry."

Seth's hand tightened on the axe handle. A primal sort of fear nestled in his guts. He tried to not breathe too loud in case it provoked the wolves. He watched them through the falling snow.

The face-off lasted less than two minutes. The alpha turned away from the men and trotted to the other side of the street, the rest of the pack following in order, watching all the time.

Soon they vanished into the white fog, like ashen ghosts in a peculiar dream.

CHAPTER FOURTEEN

Moving through the town, they saw a serpentine monster coiled among the remains of a gutted building, and fled into nearby streets before it woke.

Tattered remnants of humanity persisted in isolated pockets, but they withdrew from sight when approached. They were wide-eyed and dirty-faced, clutching makeshift cudgels and bats. Filthy, bedraggled, and injured. Seth tried to engage with them, but to no success.

"Why won't they talk to us?" Andy said.

"They're barely managing," Weir replied.

Ruby watched the last of the ragged survivors disappear into the warren of back streets. "Maybe they're scared of the rifle. I wonder what happened to them. At least they're still alive."

"People survive," said Weir.

"God help them," Ruby muttered.

Andy glanced at the sky. "God help us all."

They walked on.

Weir led them to the hospital, which was abandoned except for a few shambling maniacs, driven mad by the terror of the last few days. Weir threatened them with his rifle to keep them away, and they retreated into darkened rooms, all gleaming eyes and cries of distress. A little later, when they ambushed the group with knives and bloodied hammers, Weir was forced to shoot them.

The police station had been taken over and fortified by armed survivors who chased the four survivors away with warning shots and sincere threats."At least there are people still alive," said Seth.

Weir looked around, disappointment on his face. "Those people don't give a shit about anyone else."

Not long after midday they left the town behind and headed for Briar Slope.

*

A mile farther on, they found the corpses of several cows lying scattered in the snow upon a country road. The cattle had been partially eaten; their throats opened, their rib cages exposed and broken, viscera trailing. Their shredded hides were half-frozen. There was no smell. Everything was covered in a fine dust of snow.

Seth looked up at a line of crows watching from upon a telephone wire. They just stared back at him until he turned away.

There were no boot prints or tracks nearby, but areas of the snow seemed to have been disturbed in mounds. When Seth looked closer at the surface of the snow, he saw shallow trails, about half a metre wide, leading away from the animal corpses.

"Something was hungry," Ruby said, chewing on her fingernail. Her other hand remained wrapped in the silver cross.

A frown darkened Weir's face as he studied the remains.

Seth stepped towards him. "What's wrong?"

"Do you hear that?" Andy said behind them. "Sounds like a low rumbling."

Weir looked at Seth, concern in his eyes, his mouth tensing. And he had barely raised his rifle when the snow around them exploded in a maelstrom of awful screeching and serpentine forms.

Seth fell back, crying out, as Weir's rifle barked several times. Snow fell and swirled all about him, finding his eyes and disorientating him. Andy and Ruby screamed from nearby. Seth pivoted to one side to see Andy struggling with something on the ground.

Weir's rifle rang out again with deafening staccato gunfire.

And then Seth saw one of the things that had erupted from the snow. It was some kind of worm-creature, limbless and segmented, as big as a dog, with red skin and an eyeless head. It emerged from the snow, reared before him, and opened its circular mouth to bare tiny, sharp teeth. The flesh around its mouth was pinkish and loosely flapping.

It lunged towards him.

He swung his axe once, screaming in a manic fugue born from trauma, and buried its blade halfway down the nightmare's abdomen. Black blood splashed in the snow and across Seth's face. The worm writhed on the end of the axe, squealing and snapping, until he raised one booted foot and stamped on its glistening head.

He wiped his face, spat the sulphuric taste of the worm's blood from his mouth, and pulled his axe free. More dead worms lay in the snow, punctured with bullets. The surviving worms burrowed into the snow and fled from Weir's rifle-fire.

Seth went to Andy, who was on his knees next to a dying worm. Ruby was slowly rising to her feet; she seemed unharmed. The worm twitched and shuddered, impaled by Andy's knife, until its heart finally stopped. Andy stared at the worm, breathing hard, and he flinched when Seth touched him on the shoulder. He blinked, opened his mouth, but said nothing. Seth and Ruby helped him up and they turned back to Weir.

There must have been over a dozen dead worms in the snow. They were scattered amongst the cattle remains. It was all...flesh.

Weir hunched over, retching and spitting. He straightened, wiped his face with his hands. His coat was streaked with black blood.

"Vicious little motherfuckers." He reloaded his rifle and stared in the direction the worms had fled. "Everyone all right?"

"Yeah," Seth and Ruby answered together. Andy nodded, wiping his mouth, his eyes damp and tired.

"We need to run," said Weir.

"What?" asked Seth. "Why?"

"Something else is coming."

CHAPTER FIFTEEN

They struggled through the snow as the giant worm rose within the white fog and let out a shockingly loud shriek that tightened Seth's bladder and took most of the strength from his legs.

"Keep moving!" Weir roared, glancing over his shoulder. The vibrations and juddering tremors in the ground threw them off-balance, and had them staggering and slipping. Seth risked a look back and wished he hadn't when he saw the mother worm turn towards them and propel itself through the snow, swiping away trees, hedgerows, thickets and fences with its massive body. It would chase them down and snaffle them up, bones and all.

"Don't stop," Weir shouted. "Don't look back! Run!"

Seth kicked his legs with all his strength, panting, each breath scraping in his throat. Andy pushed Ruby ahead and told her to keep moving. Weir urged them on from behind.

Seth was fading. He felt pathetic and overwhelmed, like an insignificant morsel for the god-mass of the giant mother worm. When Andy fell down, Seth collapsed with him, and they hit the snow in a bedraggled heap. Andy's rattling sobs were the prominent sounds in Seth's ears, before the worm shrieked again and obliterated all rational thought.

Weir and Ruby were upon them, pulling them to their feet, and they huddled in the presence of the approaching titan.

"Go on," said Weir.

Seth looked at him. "What?"

Weir handed Seth his side-arm. "Take this and go. Make a run for it and find shelter. There's a full magazine in the pistol."

"I don't know how to use it."

Weir put his hand on Seth's shoulder. "You'll figure it out." Then he turned away and aimed his rifle at the mother worm.

*

Seth, Ruby and Andy fled towards the houses ahead of them. Gunfire rattled from behind. Weir was shouting in defiance. The mother worm's shrieks shook the ground and split the sky.

The hamlet was composed of less than a dozen houses scattered about a road that curved away in a south-westerly direction. Dead street lights loomed over them as they stumbled past abandoned cars and gardens lost to snow. The houses were intact, but held a sense of desolation and emptiness about them.

They fell through a doorway, and Seth slammed it shut behind them. Just another abandoned house. Pictures and keepsakes. A family home left behind.

Under the stairs was a door that opened into the darkness of a cramped storage space. They ducked inside and closed the door. There was barely enough room for the three of them as they dropped to a crouch against the back wall of bare plaster.

They huddled together. The room smelled of musty

paper and sawdust. Seth switched on his torch, and the light revealed Andy's terrified face amid floating motes of dust. Ruby had screwed her eyes shut, and she clung to her silver cross with both hands.

Beyond the house, the sound of Weir's rifle stopped and there was just the shrieking of the mother worm. Then the walls and the floor began shaking. A pile of magazines collapsed across the floor and clay pots rattled on a shelf.

They covered their heads with their arms and hunched down as the tremors worsened, seeming to grip the house and shake its foundations.

The torch fell from Seth's grip and winked out. All was darkness. The shrieking became louder, deafening, and the sound of screaming metal filled the walls.

Seth closed his eyes and waited to die.

CHAPTER SIXTEEN

When they emerged from the room under the stairs, they found that the house's walls had partially fallen in, and a drizzle of snow was falling through the ragged holes and wide gaps where most of the roof had been.

Debris everywhere, all over the floor, the rooms smashed to bits, the inner walls barely standing. Shattered bricks and plaster. Splintered wooden beams jutting from drifts of wreckage.

They picked their way through the remains of the hallway, coughing from the brick dust, plaster granules, and grit that covered them.

The front door hung from one set of twisted hinges. Seth wrenched it back and stepped outside, Andy and Ruby right behind him. They stood looking around, aghast and shivering.

The entire hamlet was in ruins around the buckled road. The smell of sewage and gas. The snow was slowly covering this new devastation.

There was no sign of the mother worm. No sign of Weir. They called out for him, looked for him amongst the wreckage, but he wasn't to be found. Seth thought he must have been obliterated, wiped from existence.

Andy stood on the broken road, nudging fragments of tarmac with his foot, an appalled pallor on his face. He was weeping.

Ruby went to him and held his hand, neither of them

saying a word. Seth stood with them. Then all three of them moved on.

*

"How far to your village, Seth?" Andy asked, breathing raggedly. Seth had given him the axe. Ruby hummed the slow tune of some old song.

They walked a narrow road hemmed in by thin trees. Their boots scraped through the snow.

"Not far," Seth said. He kept one hand on the pistol buried deep in the pocket of his coat. His feet were freezing and his trembling guts forced bile into his chest. And in that moment, shaking with cold, the mere thought of the warmth of the sun on his face, of the warmth of his parents' embrace, almost brought him to his knees.

"Do you think Weir's dead?"

Seth didn't answer. He couldn't answer.

"He was a good man," Andy added.

"Yes, he was."

"I'd pray for Weir, if I still believed in God." Andy seemed to remember Ruby's silver cross, and glanced across to her as she walked beside him. "Sorry, I didn't mean to offend or anything."

Ruby looked at him. "It's fine. I'm not offended. And even if I was, what would it matter now, in this new world? There are graver things to worry about."

Andy dropped his gaze to the snow. "Fair enough. I just meant, uh..."

"It doesn't matter."

"Okay."

Ruby shook her head. "I've been asking myself a question ever since this started."

"What question?" Seth said.

"Why would God let this happen?"

"That's a good question. Have you found an answer?"

"I'm not sure I want to find one."

"It's something to think about, I suppose," said Andy.

"I don't want to think about it."

"Oh, I'm sorry."

She offered him a slight smile. "Stop saying you're sorry, Andy."

Moments later the road sign for Seth's village coalesced out the white fog ahead of them. It was furred with snow, tilting to one side.

BRIAR SLOPE - 1 mile

They moved past the sign, and half an hour later the blurred shapes of houses at the outskirts of the village soon appeared from the veil of swirling snow.

"Here we are," Seth said. "We made it. We fucking made it."

CHAPTER SEVENTEEN

Before the snow, the village had been home to over one thousand people, but now it stood deserted and derelict. This was Briar Slope, where he was born on a summer's night in 1992. Where memories both good and bad were gathered and guarded like treasure.

They walked the main road into the village, stepping around wreckage and debris. They climbed over a fallen tree trunk.

Something of great size had passed through Briar Slope and cut a path of devastation, leaving many houses destroyed. There were bodies and splintered bones in the snow. Ripped clothes and rags hanging on the limbs of the trees that were still standing.

"Oh my God," Andy whispered, looking around with wide eyes. The axe shook in his hand. In silence Ruby gawped at the destruction.

Reluctantly, Seth pulled Weir's pistol from his pocket and held it facing the ground. He kept his finger away from the trigger. Bile frothed behind his sternum. He wanted to vomit, and tremors ran up his arms.

They walked past the village shop, which was burnt to carbon and cinders.

Farther on, they sighted an old man in a trench coat sitting on a wooden bench at one side of the street. He watched them approach, and gave a pitiful smile as they stopped. He noted Seth's pistol and shrugged.

"Hello," Andy said, staying protectively close to Ruby.

"Hello," the man replied. His eyes were watery and rimmed with pinkish skin. "Just passing through?"

"I live here," said Seth.

"One of the monsters passed through here, as you can see."

"Was it a giant worm?" Andy asked.

The man wiped his mouth. "No, not that one. It was something different. A god, you might say. An eater of souls and flesh." He exhaled, his breath shuddering. "Most of the remaining people - those who hadn't disappeared in the snow - had already evacuated for the coasts. But there were still a few of us left when it arrived. I was the only one to survive." He said this last statement with something like pride, a twitch of a smile at the side of his mouth. The man's insanity gleamed in the light of his eyes but Seth suddenly recognised the man. It was almost funny.

"I know you. Your name is Alec Palmer. You used to be the village butcher, before you passed the shop on to your son."

The man frowned, spat over his shoulder. "That was my old life. My son and his family are gone. Now I show the way to those who pass through here."

"What does that mean?"

"I tell people about the monsters. I tell them about the crossing of worlds."

"Of course you do," Andy said dismissively, keeping the axe half-raised. "You're as mad as a bucket of frogs."

Palmer snorted. "Probably. But what other choice is

there but to be mad in a world of gods and monsters?"

No one answered him. Seth even agreed a little with him and found some sympathy for the man.

"I will see the extinction of Man," Palmer said, and then he rose from the bench on stiff legs and stretched his arms.

Seth, Ruby and Andy stepped back a little.

"Good luck," Palmer said, and walked off in the direction they had come from, to disappear in the falling snow.

*

Soon afterwards they arrived at Seth's house and stood before it in the street, staring at its remains. The front wall of the house was in pieces on the lawn and scattered around the driveway. The roof had caved in, and the rooms were wrecked.

Seth found it hard to swallow, as if his throat was stuffed with dirt and sand. His heart ached and crashed. His legs went all watery as panic and wretched dread filled him up.

Andy put his hand on Seth's shoulder. "I'm so sorry, man."

"I have to know," Seth said. "I have to know." Shrugging off Andy's hand, he stepped over the buckled garden gate to search for his parents amongst the ruins.

He found their ravaged, frozen corpses sprawled together beneath a large piece of debris. Their faces were obscured by smashed bricks and mortar, and for that he was almost relieved.

Seth kneeled down and put his hands over his face and cried for a long while.

*

"Do you want to bury them?" Ruby asked him, her voice low and soft in the cold air.

Seth took his hands from his face and wiped his eyes dry. He shuddered out a breath. "Best to leave them; they're together, for what it's worth. And I don't think I could drag them out from under the debris."

Ruby recovered a blanket from the ruins, and Seth draped it over his parents' remains. Afterwards Ruby went back out to the street and stood with Andy on the pavement, while Seth considered whether to search the wreckage of his home for any personal effects. But in the end, all he could bring himself to recover from the ruins were a few photos, before turning away, unable to look at the house any longer. And after he'd said goodbye to his old home and his parents, he walked out to the street and stood beside Andy and Ruby.

"What shall we do, now?" Andy said.

Seth looked up and down the street, along the rows of broken houses. The church had lost its steeple.

Somewhere beyond the village, terrible beasts wailed and cried in the wastelands.

CHAPTER EIGHTEEN

Andy wrapped his arms over his chest and shivered in the cold. "Maybe we should find somewhere to stay for the night, before anything else passes through here."

Seth bowed his head. "I don't want to stay in the village."

"But we won't survive in the dark out in the snow and fog," replied Andy. "Please, Seth. We need to find shelter."

Ruby looked about the street, her teeth chattering. She rubbed her arms. "Andy's right."

Seth's mouth felt sore as he let out a prolonged breath. He made sure not to turn back to see the devastation of his house. So many memories back there. But memories wouldn't do him any good. He raised his face to Andy.

"All right. Lead the way."

*

At the outskirts of the village they found an intact house not yet compromised by any kind of creature. It stood at the top of a gentle rise in the ground, with no tracks around it, near a grove of trees. The front door was unlocked, the insides neat and untouched by any violence or disorder.

They didn't bother to barricade the doors or block the windows. They were exhausted - and if some giant entity passed through it would smash the house to bits anyway. There was no protection.

Everything seemed so paltry and forlorn.

Seth just wanted to sleep. He felt hollowed out and useless, beyond help. All he could do was lie on the sofa and stare at the opposite wall. He didn't care or even wonder about the people who once lived in the house. He ignored the photographs on the shelves. Trembling seized his arms and his hands. He couldn't eat.

Andy and Ruby sat within a nest of blankets on the thick carpet of the living room, sharing a packet of crisps that rustled in their shaking hands.

The snow fell against the house.

It was still daylight when they fell into a deep sleep of exhaustion.

*

No refuge in his dreams. No comfort in the faces of the dead people he once knew. Nothing but monsters and bloodthirsty gods.

*

In the morning, Seth woke cold, groggy and aching-limbed. Andy and Ruby were looking out of the living room window.

"Someone's out there," Ruby said. "There are lights."

Seth sat up, rubbed his head. "Lights?"

Andy glanced back at him. "Out past the snow, in the fog. Maybe a car or something."

With a tired grunt, Seth rose shakily from the sofa, keeping the blankets draped over his shoulders as he went to the window. He cleared his throat and sagged on his sore feet.

He didn't see the lights at first; his vision was still blurry from sleep and stinging with tiredness. But then twin beams of headlights appeared within the white fog and moved towards the house.

They stumbled outside, into the driving snow. Seth's eyes smarted from the cold air. The wind flailed at the survivors, tried to drive them back to the doorway, but they dug their feet in and struggled towards the headlights.

"There it is," Andy shouted. He flicked on his torch and pointed it towards the approaching lights, then he worked the switch to make the torch beam blink repeatedly as a makeshift signal. Seth waved his arms and called out, his voice rasping and dry. Ruby stood in silence, her hands at her face, wavering in the cold.

The headlights neared, creeping closer and growing brighter, until the sound of a slow, rattling engine could be heard.

Seth put his arms down. Andy grimaced into the wailing wind and stood closer to Ruby. The growling of the engine rose above the wind, and the shape of a large green tractor emerged upon the road, clearing a path for itself with a curved snowplough attached to its front. Its huge wheels were bulky and thickly-grooved, clotted with snow. A shadowed figure sat inside the cab.

"Holy shit," Andy said. There was awe in his voice.

"We've been saved," muttered Ruby. "Thank God."

The tractor was pulling a long, open-top trailer that bore a makeshift roof of tarpaulin sheets held up by thin lengths of wood and tent poles. Within the trailer, the huddled forms of over two dozen survivors looked up or turned their heads to stare at Seth, Ruby and Andy from beneath their swaddled blankets, coats and stained duvets. Children peered over the raised side of the trailer. Dirty, unwashed, desperate. Lost souls, all.

CHAPTER NINETEEN

They left the house behind, and Seth looked back at the vanishing shape of the village as the tractor moved along the road. He gave a silent goodbye to his parents.

The three of them sat at the rear of the trailer, awkward in the presence of strangers. The trailer shuddered over the wide road, whose lines and angles were only hinted at beneath the snow. There was the smell of old sweat and neglect, mixed with the faint odour of animal dung. The tarpaulin canopy flapped above them. The wind pushed at the trailer, sweeping about in gusts that seemed to speak if Seth listened too intently.

The trailer was crammed with people, scattered supplies of food, water, equipment and clothes, all vaguely chaotic in the huddling of survivors clad in winter clothes and woollen hats. Some of the people bore wounds and injuries. A few looked ill. Traumatised hearts and minds.

Seth looked around, but the others avoided eye contact, except for a few children who watched him warily. He tried to smile at them, but couldn't maintain the shape of his mouth. His expression became more of an aggrieved grimace. He noticed makeshift weapons clutched in hands or lying on the grimy floor of the trailer. There were hammers, an axe, assorted lengths of lead pipe, a crowbar, and a baseball bat. A man, wearing an oversized coat and a furred cap with ear flaps, sat on a plastic lawn chair, his back to everyone else as he looked out from the trailer, keeping watch. He cradled a double-barrelled shotgun across his chest. His darkly-stubbled face was flecked with snow, his eyes squinting, mouth tight with a scowl.

In the tractor cab, Quinn hunched behind the steering wheel, keeping the tractor in the middle of the road. He was a middle-aged man in layers of winter clothing. Perched behind and to the side of him, his brother Mack held a bolt-action hunting rifle with a telescopic sight atop it. Mack kept glancing back at Seth, no expression on his haggard face. His eyes were the colour of dark soil.

Seth looked away from him. He recalled the two men climbing down from the cab when the tractor arrived at the house. They had appraised Seth, Ruby and Andy, asking them questions in a vaguely threatening manner. They had let Seth keep the axe, but he'd been forced to hand over his pistol. Seth hadn't protested, and was glad to be rid of the firearm. He didn't trust himself with it, and the two men seemed competent with guns - they had that look about them. Proper countryside types, who lived close to the earth and cared little for the outside world of large towns and urban sprawls.

Quinn had taken the pistol and pocketed it. Then the brothers invited them to join the others in the trailer. It hadn't taken long for Seth, Ruby, and Andy to decide.

And now they were on the road, heading north to an army base rumoured to be taking in survivors.

Andy hunched over, smoking a cigarette. No one seemed to mind the smoke, especially Ruby, who sat especially close to him with her arm hooked around his.

An old woman to Seth's right sat against the side of the trailer, and she caught his eye with an anxious smile. A grey blanket draped over her shoulders. She was holding a sleeping baby, no more than six months old and swaddled in blankets.

"I'm Delia," she said. She looked to be in her sixties or seventies.

Seth gave her his name. Andy and Ruby nodded at Delia.

"Where are we heading exactly?" Seth asked the woman. "Quinn told us that we're going to an army base up north. Where up north?"

"Somewhere in Staffordshire," Delia said, one hand brushing loose strands of greasy hair behind one ear. Her face told of the last few days of struggle. "We've been picking up survivors here and there. Quinn and Mack rescued me from Dorchester. They're good men. They saved us all."

Delia noticed Seth glance at the baby.

"He's my grandson," she said. "His name's Jack. Such a lovely boy." She kissed him on the forehead.

"Where are his parents?" Seth immediately regretted asking the question, and even more so when he saw the glimmer of pain in Delia's face.

"They died in Dorchester. Killed by one of those godawful monsters. I managed to save Jack and get away. Now, I feel guilty."

"Because you couldn't save his parents?"

"My daughter and her husband. I couldn't do anything. I feel like I let them die."

"You're only human. At least Jack is safe. I'm sure they'd be grateful to you for that."

Delia gave a slight nod without much conviction.

"I'm sorry," Seth said. "I shouldn't have asked."

"It's fine. Gotta keep going for Jack."

"That's admirable."

"I'm all he's got left. He's all *I've* got left. I'm not going to fail him."

No one spoke for a while. The snowfall dwindled to a stop, but the sky was darkening in slow degrees. Seth wondered if it would ever rain again.

"Does anyone even know what caused all this?" Andy said. "Where do the monsters come from?"

"I've heard stories," Delia said. "Hearsay."

Andy extinguished his cigarette and threw it out of the trailer. "What kind of hearsay?"

Delia sniffled, wiped her nose on the back of her hand. She pulled the swaddled blankets tighter around Jack's sleeping form and looked at the two men. "I heard someone say that the monsters are from Hell - the manifestations of humanity's sins. Sins made into flesh. Sounds bloody ridiculous, if you ask me."

Ruby frowned at Delia, and blinked.

"You believe that?" asked Seth.

"I don't believe Hell is real," she answered. "But I believe we're in some version of it, for the foreseeable future. Apart from that, I have no idea."

Andy sighed and sat back. "My grandfather was very religious, and he always said that Hell was a place of deep cold, not fire and brimstone. I know it sounds crazy, but this feels like the Hell he talked about."

"Christ," said Seth, wiping his mouth. He noticed Ruby

turn away to hide her face.

Delia gazed down at her grandson with a trembling smile. "Christ is gone, I think."

The baby boy slept, blissfully oblivious to the world that wanted to consume him.

CHAPTER TWENTY

The tractor pushed through rising drifts upon the road, weaving between snow-clotted car wrecks and around pile-ups. Its tyres fought for purchase, occasionally slipping and skidding over the more treacherous parts. The sounds of its engine and stuttering exhaust echoed into the snow and white fog.

Seth wondered how many bodies were lost beneath the snow. He and Andy peered over the side of the trailer at a single-engine aircraft that had crash-landed on the roadside. It was crumpled and broken within a grove of blackened trees. Human remains hung from the upper branches of a leafy birch. Limbs and viscera dangled like decorations.

Food was shared amongst the survivors. Delia fed Jack from a bottle of Cow & Gate instant milk. Seth watched them, amazed that such a vulnerable thing was surviving the cataclysm. He thought about the sacrifices and hardships there would be just to keep that little life from being snuffed out by the cold. To protect that tiny spark in a world of darkness. He thought about the problems ahead. He thought about the survival of children.

Someone told a joke.

Later on, the tractor stopped and several of the people disembarked from the trailer, clutching handfuls of toilet paper, and warily moving into a dense thicket. Mack stood guard at the vehicle with his hunting rifle, while men and women with makeshift weapons watched the road and the surrounding area.

Seth took two wads of tissue and went to shit behind a patch of overgrown nettles. As he relieved himself, he heard distant roaring to the east, and when he emerged from the trees the other refugees were staring up at the massive gliding silhouette of something that resembled a giant stingray.

Ruby stood near him, her eyes wide. "It's beautiful and terrible."

Before the flying thing vanished deeper into the low clouds, a squirming form was glimpsed struggling in its hanging claws. It looked a lot like a person.

Ruby looked at Seth then turned away.

They were all prey now. Animals to be hunted.

*

They travelled for the rest of the day, and when the light began to fade they took shelter for the night at an old barn, not far from the road. Seth had been one of the men and women who'd checked the building was safe before the rest of the group was allowed inside. His hands had been shaking around the axe haft the entire time. Then the supplies were brought in and placed in the middle of the floor. People made spaces for rest and sleeping around the edges and up in the hayloft. Coleman lanterns were lit and camping stoves fired up to cook a communal meal of baked beans and tinned sausages.

The few children played simple games away from the adults

Seth's little group found some space near a rusting piece of farm machinery and sat on the hard-packed dirt floor waiting for the food to be ready. Delia sat nearby, cooing to Jack, who gurgled and whined. The barn smelled of mildew, old wood, and dust.

The steaming food was dished out in paper bowls, with plastic forks and knives. Cheese crackers and chunks of chocolate were given to the younger ones as a treat. They ate in a loose gathering, mostly in silence. The walls creaked around them. The wind rose to a distressed wail, pushing at the old building as if to test its strength and fortitude. Quinn said that they might have to dig out the tractor and trailer in the morning, depending on how heavy the snow was overnight.

When they had finished their meals, they gathered the bowls and cutlery in a pile and retired to their makeshift beds of blankets, sleeping bags and duvets. A red-haired woman with a long knife fixed to her belt read stories to the children.

Andy was already snoring gently, at peace for a few precious hours. Ruby slept beside him. Delia sat nearby and rocked Jack to sleep, then returned him to his crib of blankets and lay down next to it. Her eyes flicked towards Seth, and he nodded at her. She returned the small gesture.

He rubbed his eyes and yawned. He shivered, more from grief than cold. Exhaustion was a slow pulse within him. He thought of his parents and missed them terribly. Bad memories of his teenage years, when he hadn't been a good son, made his face burn with shame and his heart crumple. He regretted every argument and angry word. He wished he could have made them proud of him.

"Sorry," he whispered, with tears in his eyes. No one heard him.

Seth lay down, staring at the glowing Coleman lantern

in the middle of the barn. He passed into a sleep filled with nightmares.

CHAPTER TWENTY-ONE

In the morning Seth woke to panicked voices and found that a boy had gone missing during the night. His father was on the verge of hysteria; two men were holding him back from going outside alone. He swore and spat, said he had to find his boy, and was only calmed by Quinn's decision to send out a small group to search for his son.

"I've already lost my wife," he said. "I can't lose Grant as well."

"Was he taken by something?" asked Mack.

Quinn shook his head. "I found the door left open when I woke this morning, and his tracks in the snow leading away. There was no blood."

"We have to get out there and find him," the father said. "We have to get out there *now*."

"Yes, we will," said Quinn. "No one gets left behind."

"Let's get it done," said Mack. He would lead the group out into the snow. Seth volunteered so he'd have something to distract him from thoughts of his parents. The rest of the group was made up of the father - whose name was Neal - and two other men, Darren and Callum. Darren was a wiry man with reddened eyes. Callum was the man in the furry Russian hat with ear flaps; he stared out from the doorway, gripping his shotgun, as the others got ready for the search.

Seth took his axe. Mack readied his hunting rifle, while Neal and Darren each carried a knife.

"Good luck," Andy said to Seth.

"Thanks," Seth replied. His heart was clattering. Adrenaline drained his mouth of saliva and soured his throat. He shifted on his feet to disguise the shaking of his legs.

Delia watched from nearby, rocking baby Jack in her arms. She looked pale and wan, older than she had appeared yesterday.

"Come on, let's go," Neal said, panic and worry in his face. His eyes were watery and bloodshot. He took gulping breaths. "We can't leave him out there."

Mack led the men outside. Seth and Neal walked either side of him, while Darren and Callum walked behind. The tractor and trailer were parked nearby and appeared untouched.

The boy's footprints trailed away from the barn and to the east. The men stood scanning their surroundings, grimacing in the falling snow. The wind howled high above them. Seth thought he heard the deep growling of thunder from far away, followed by distant crashes that could have been the impact of falling trees.

Mack crouched beside the tracks, looked down at them. "They're fresh. The boy hasn't been gone long. There are no other tracks." He looked up at Neal. "Do you have any idea why he'd leave?"

Neal rubbed at his face. "I'm not sure. He never spoke a word yesterday. And sometimes he just...uh, loses track of what's going on. He hasn't been the same since his mother was killed."

"That's not surprising, is it?" said Callum.

Darren nodded, as if it was needed.

"We have to hurry," Neal said, his mouth trembling as he looked at Grant's tracks going off into the white fog. "He needs our help. Oh God. My poor boy, out there all alone."

"We'll find him," said Mack. "He couldn't have gone far."

Neal was already following his son's tracks. The other men pulled up their hoods and moved after him.

*

They stayed close together, keeping watch with weapons ready. The snow was coming down harder than it had done when they'd left the barn. Sweeping winds ghosted over them.

Mack and Neal walked either side of Grant's tracks. Seth held his axe with both hands, and he looked out for the lost boy. He winced at the cold working its way into his aching bones. His teeth chattered. He glanced back to see Darren hunching over and wiping at his face. Callum had his shotgun raised and ready for anything that came out of the white fog and falling snow.

Neal began calling out for his son with his hands cupped to his mouth. His voice was hoarse and panicked.

Through several fields they kept following the tracks, scared and hyper-alert. They'd lost sight of the barn in the distance behind them, and Seth worried that if their tracks were swept away by the wind or buried in the falling snow, they wouldn't be able to find their way back. There were many different deaths waiting for them in the cold wastelands.

A few minutes later, they found a small woollen hat discarded on a patch of bloodstained snow. The blood was half-frozen. *Recent.* The tracks stopped at the hat.

The group halted. Each man stared down at the hat and the spread of wet red upon and around it.

Neal seemed to become breathless, clutching his chest with one hand. He dropped his knife and collapsed to his knees on the snow, then let out a braying sob that descended into shuddering breaths of grief and pain.

The other men regarded each other, their faces pale and forlorn. Darren stared at the blood. Callum shook his head, his eyes downcast in the frail light.

Neal picked up his son's hat in both hands and held it close to his face. With futile hope he looked about for any other sign of Grant, but the boy was gone. Completely gone. He slumped, sobbing with his head bowed and the sodden, bloodied hat at his face muffling his cries.

"Christ," Mack muttered, looking away.

Darren doubled over to dry-heave, and then fell into a coughing fit until Callum slapped him on the back. He straightened, wiping his watery eyes.

"What do you think did it?" Seth asked, and immediately regretted the question.

"Doesn't matter," Mack said quietly.

"The boy's gone," said Callum, as a gurgling roar drifted out of the distance. "We should go back. There's nothing out here for us."

Mack glanced at Neal, still crying on his knees and oblivious to them all. He stepped over and placed his hand on his shoulder, but Neal shrugged him off and stood, then turned to face the rest of the group with tears down his face.

"We failed him. My boy. My wonderful boy. Such a wonderful boy." Neal looked down at the hat in his hands, gripping it between his fingers, the last remnant of his son.

"We need to go back, Neal," said Mack. "I'm so sorry. But he's gone, and we have to get back to the barn. It's not safe to be out here."

"You're not sorry," Neal said, meeting the eyes of each man standing before him. "None of you are." His shoulders shook with anger and grief, the rest of his body tensing and clenched as if he were suppressing a scream.

"You have my deepest sympathies," Mack said to him. "But we can't stay out here."

Neal's voice was barely heard. "All those years for nothing. The years we lived, meaningless. All for a lonely death in the cold."

Mack took another step towards him. "Let's get you back to the barn, my friend."

Neal seemed to contemplate Mack's words, blinking away tears and flecks of snow. Then he nodded and started to move towards Mack.

The next few moments happened very fast, and there was nothing to be done.

A giant shape, with spiked wings spread wide, coalesced within the low clouds above them and started down towards the men in a swift swoop. It was some kind of albino bat, approximately eight feet tall, with a wingspan of approximately twice that, and red eyes set within a sunken, squat face of pale fur and pinkish skin, topped by pointed ears upon its head. Its abdomen was covered in sore tumours and cysts amidst the wispy white hair, which was matted in places with dried blood. A nightmare vision with broad wings threaded with scarlet veins and capillaries. Its mouth was wet and awful, and full of killing teeth as it shrieked and fell upon Neal, grabbing him by his shoulders and plucking him from the ground. His cries of agony rose into a shrill wailing as the bat struggled to lift him higher into the sky. Its claws tightened upon him. He dropped Grant's hat.

Mack and Callum raised their weapons. Seth grabbed Darren and pulled him back.

Neal was still screaming when the giant bat swung its head forward and bit down upon the top of his skull. Its mouth gnashed and ripped until his struggles stopped and most of his face was gone. Neal's arms twitched. Blood fountained from the debris of his head and fell upon the snow. His left eye was gone, somewhere in the bat's mouth or already in its stomach, and the remaining one had turned upwards in its wrecked socket. His exposed brain glistened, half-shredded within the cradle of his skull.

The bat raised its gore-streaked face and shrieked at the other men. Its long pink tongue unravelled and emerged, writhing and flicking, dripping saliva.

Callum stepped forward and emptied both barrels of his shotgun at the creature. Mack fired his rifle, worked the bolt, and fired again.

The bat screamed and roared in the brief hail of buckshot and bullets. It dropped Neal's body and flapped its wings, lifting away into the white fog and low clouds. Mack fired again before the creature disappeared, and he kept his rifle aimed upwards, ready for it to descend again.

Seth stared at Neal's body; the man had died while

grieving for his son. His last moments must have been torture before the bat's horrid mouth had finished him.

Seth thought of his own father and suppressed a sob. Darren vomited nearby. Callum reloaded his shotgun without once taking his gaze from the sky.

Mack only looked once at Neal before turning away and facing the others. "Back to the barn, before that fucking thing returns."

"What about Neal?" Darren said, wiping his mouth and breathing hard.

"We leave him," Mack replied. "His troubles are over."

CHAPTER TWENTY-TWO

The men struggled through the snow, and were less than two hundred metres from the barn when another monster emerged, drawn by the gunfire and raised voices. It came from their right side, loping on several dozen insectile legs, all double-jointed and sharp-tipped. A bloated thing of pallid flesh - as big as an elephant - with four long, crooked arms that ended in snapping crab claws.

Its face was all teeth within a red mouth.

The men tried to outrun the creature. Callum emptied his shotgun at it, with little effect. Mack fired his rifle.

Darren was running beside Seth, and then he was gone, snatched up by one of the creature's claws. He screamed only once, before the creature snipped him in half at the waist and then stuffed the upper part of him into its mouth. Seth glanced back to see it all, panic and fear leaving him witless, everything chaotic around him. Callum fired his shotgun again. More shots from Mack's rifle.

The bloated creature screeched.

Seth was only fifty metres from the barn, when something barrelled into him from his left side and flattened him. He lay sprawling on his back, the air knocked out his lungs, hurting from the collision and breathing hard through gritted teeth. He patted himself down to make sure nothing was broken.

A low hiss from behind caused him to tilt his head back to see what new horror awaited him.

From his upside down view, he saw something like a flayed bull standing several strides away from him. It was about the size of a tiger or lion, its skinless form twitching, chattering through the sharp teeth in its mouth. Black claws scraped at the snow. It snorted, its jaundice-hued eyes set upon Seth, sizing him up for another attack.

He scrambled to his feet, standing with his legs slightly bent and his hands held out. The axe was on the ground about two metres to his left, but he didn't dare move to retrieve it.

Seth froze as the thing snarled and broke into a charge. Fear paralysed him. He didn't even scream.

Glass shattered upon the creature, and flames erupted upon its left side. It roared, stumbling and blinded. Seth dove out of its way, the flames licking at his back. The creature collapsed, thrashing in the snow, making a horrid choking sound as it was burned to ruin. It only stilled when Quinn stepped over and shot it in the skull with his pistol.

"Thank you," said Seth, his breath stuttering out of him.

Quinn nodded.

It had all happened in less than a minute.

Seth climbed to his feet, brushing snow from his coat. Mack and Callum stood next to him. They looked worn out and half-mad. Seth glanced around for the other beast, but there was no sign of it.

"It's gone," Mack said to him, reloading his rifle. "Must have had its fill with Darren."

Seth put his hands to his face. "Darren. Oh God."

"No time to fuck around," said Mack. "He's gone. Neal

and his son are gone. We have to get back on the road."

CHAPTER TWENTY-THREE

The survivors headed north, and some said prayers for the dead. Quinn had refuelled the tractor before they left the barn. They were down to their last can of diesel, but the brothers said it should be enough to reach the army base. If they were lying, they hid it well.

The snow fell for another hour then stopped, and it was a welcome respite for the people in the trailer, even with the dubious shelter of the tarpaulin sheets. But soon it began to fall again.

The snowplough made a path and nudged aside the occasional car wreck blocking the way. A plume of grey smoke rose from the tractor's chimney exhaust. The plough and the tractor's wheel's kicked up snow in a grainy spray that added to the drifting downpour.

Seth sat with his knees drawn to his chest, his arms around them, and he rocked and shook with the motion of the trailer. He thought about all the deaths he'd seen. He thought about his parents and their final resting place. He thought the world was without hope.

Farther on, Ruby and Andy brought to his attention the corpses at the roadsides. All twisted and frozen in their death throes. Entire families lost to the cold.

"Refugees," said Ruby.

"Just like us," Andy muttered. "Poor bastards."

Seth said nothing and turned away.

*

The tractor trundled past a farmhouse whose roof had collapsed to leave the four walls barely standing. Outhouses and barns gutted and smashed. Broken structures and toppled bricks. And from within the ruins rose a behemoth of fleshy-pink tentacles, with an undulating central mass of pulsating flesh and gaping maws that reached fifty metres into the air.

Mack aimed his rifle, but he did not fire. Someone muttered a prayer. The people in the trailer stared at the massive beast as it released a haunting, whale-like cry into the sky. But it did not move from its nest amidst the ruins, and soon the tractor left it behind.

*

They were trying to find a route onto the M5 motorway when they were stopped by an accidental blockade of abandoned vehicles and fallen trees across the road. There was no way through, so they doubled back and found another way onto the motorway, but they'd lost a good hour in the process.

"We just have to follow this road all the way to Staffordshire," said Delia, cuddling Jack as he burped out the gas from his last feed. She sat across from Seth and Andy. "Sounds simple, doesn't it?"

"I wish it was," Andy said.

Ruby sat beside him and nodded. Then she looked at Seth. "You all right?"

Seth nodded once, wincing at deep pains in his leg muscles. His toes were numb. He breathed into his cupped hands then took them from his mouth. "I'll manage. I just keep thinking about what else could be out there."

"The monsters?" Delia said. Jack had fallen asleep.

"I dread to think what's waiting for us to find. The things I've seen..."

Delia held Jack tighter to her chest, and she looked at the trailer floor. "The things we've all seen. Terrible things."

"How many people have been eaten?" Seth asked. "This is insanity. I keep thinking that I should wake up, so everything can return to normal." He nodded towards Jack's sleeping form. "What kind of world will he grow up in? A world filled with monsters? Is that the future that waits for all the children?"

"This might be over soon," Delia said. "The snow might go away. It might thaw." Her eyes were watery. She didn't look convinced.

Seth recalled the image of the giant albino bat that had eaten Neal's head. "I don't know." He could feel Andy and Delia watching him, but he avoided their gazes and just looked at his knees. His bruises smarted, tender and soft, dark as ink on the skin under his clothes. His ribs ached from the collision with the flayed canine-thing Quinn had saved him from. He was constantly worried about frostbite, and the thought of his fingers and toes blackening made him feel nauseated and sullen with despair.

"People have died to save us," said Seth, shaking his head. "I haven't done anything special to survive so far; all I've done is run and hide while better people have given their lives."

"If that's the case," Ruby said, "then we need to stay

alive to make their sacrifice worth it."

Andy nodded. "Miles. Weir. All the people who died on the train. All of the dead. We owe it to them."

*

They'd been on the motorway for two miles when Seth saw the silhouettes of human figures watching from within the white fog in an adjacent field. He'd only raised his head over the side of the trailer to vomit pale grease and bile. And his breath caught in his throat at the sight of the tall, thin forms, five of them in total, standing close together with their long arms at their sides. They were indistinct, ethereal, like grey shadows. Then they faded into the fog and were gone.

No one else had seen them, so he kept the sighting to himself.

*

Later, when the snow fell heavy and fast, Quinn was forced to stop the tractor as a colossal spider crab with immense, jointed limbs crossed the motorway in the middle distance. Its exoskeleton was gnarled, ragged, and blood-red. The ground trembled as the pointed tips of the monster's spindly legs thudded upon the earth. It was as tall as a skyscraper, roaming the land for morsels. Unnervingly gangly. Something that denied all natural law. Something to end the Age of Man. Its hooting cry, and the clacking of its pincers must have carried for miles.

As the refugees watched, it passed out of sight, moving east into the veil of falling snow, and they hoped to never see it again.

*

An elderly woman died later that day. Her weak heart had failed. She'd gone peacefully, without anyone noticing at first. She was left at the roadside under a hasty covering of snow Quinn and Mack shovelled over her.

No one knew her name.

*

The land was being lost to the snow. A few people suffered with rasping coughs and dripping noses. They were all worn out and stressed. A man complained incessantly about his sore throat until someone found him a packet of soothing lozenges from the supply stock.

The children played simple games to entertain themselves. An old woman muttered the words of a hymn. Callum sharpened his survival knife, staring at his busy hands the entire time, a faraway look in his eyes.

The light began to fade. Darkness was near.

*

Dusk was falling by the time Quinn found an exit from the motorway, and when they arrived at the nearest village it was nearly full dark. The village was snowbound, and the houses showed no sign of habitation. Empty places. Abandoned.

"The snow took the people," one woman whispered.

The other refugees kept an expectant silence.

The tractor's headlights pierced the dense veil of falling snow in the darkness, revealing sagging cars reduced to blunt shapes on either side of the street. Seth and Andy stood in the trailer, holding onto the side, looking out from beneath the shelter of the tarpaulin. Seth shivered at the thought of dead people in lightless rooms.

Callum stood next to Seth, squinting and frowning. He chewed on a sweet that made his breath smell of strawberry. Other people murmured inside the trailer as torches were switched on.

"The place looks intact," Callum said. "No monsters." He cleared his throat. "No giant ones, anyway." Then he moved away, stepping between the people staring out at the street.

No one was home.

*

Quinn halted the tractor out the front of the community hall, but he kept the engine running while Mack and two other men went to search the building, weapons and torches in hand.

Five minutes later they emerged and gave the all clear. Quinn guided the tractor around the side of the building, beneath the shelter of a large tree, and switched off the engine. Silence all around, in the houses and streets. The slow falling of the snow in this bleak place. A haunted place.

The people disembarked from the trailer to take refuge for the night.

CHAPTER TWENTY-FOUR

They secured the community hall as best they could and stationed guards at the front and back doors, while Mack kept a solitary watch from the roof with his rifle. The curtains were drawn to hide the glow of lanterns and candles.

The children were settled in the back corner of the main room, while the adults picked their own spaces on the floor. Seth went through the cupboards in the small kitchen just off the main room and found a jar of coffee and one of hot chocolate. He added the items to the group's supplies.

A low murmur flowed through the room. The wind howled outside, sweeping past the windows. Hands and feet were checked for frostbite, and various injuries and ailments were tended. Food was cooked. The communal meal was eaten while people shared sad stories and told bad jokes. There was a little laughter, guarded and reluctant, petering out after a few seconds. After the meal Andy helped Delia prepare Jack for bedtime, while Seth went to look for Quinn.

He found him at the back of the hall, talking to a woman about the various people in the group who were suffering illness.

When Quinn was done, he turned to Seth, one hand sweeping at the stubble on his shaven head as he sighed deeply. He looked tired and stressed, haggard and pale. His greying beard reached down to his chest, and was still damp with melting snow.

"You OK, Seth? Something wrong?"

Seth hesitated, swallowed a nervous knot in his throat. He put his hands in his pockets. "Uh, I just wanted to thank you for saving my life this morning, outside the barn."

"It was no bother, lad," Quinn said. "No need to thank me." He seemed a little embarrassed.

"Well, I thought I should. Seemed like the right thing to do."

Quinn nodded, scratched at his beard. "You seem like a good bloke, Seth. Maybe if I'm about to be eaten by some horrible beast you can repay the favour."

Seth almost smiled, but the muscles hurt in his face. "Of course."

Quinn shrugged, glancing around at the refugees inside the main room. "We all need to look out for each other. It's the only way we'll survive this."

"I agree," said Seth. "I'm just glad that you found us."

"The more people we find," said Quinn, "the more we save from the cold." He lowered his voice. "I'll try my hardest to get everyone to the army base, but we'll lose more people before we arrive. I've accepted that. Casualties are inevitable."

The pit of Seth's stomach dipped. He prayed that if he were to die out there in the cold, it'd be a quick, and without too much pain.

Quinn said, "Would you mind taking some food up to Mack on the roof? He'll be down here to complain at me if I don't send something up to him soon. Younger brothers, eh? I love the bastard to bits, but he doesn't half bloody moan when the mood takes him."

"No worries."

"Make sure you wrap up warm before you go," said Quinn.

CHAPTER TWENTY-FIVE

Along with the food, Quinn gave Seth a bottle of whiskey. He told him not to let Mack drink it all. Seth went through the doorway towards the back of the hall and into the corridor that led to the throat of stairs. He switched on his torch and climbed to the first floor, which was used to store random equipment and furniture. Seth noticed a ping-pong table next to one wall. A pile of cardboard boxes. A tall cupboard, its doors open, revealed dusty cleaning supplies.

He went up the ladder, opened the roof hatch, and emerged with the snow and darkness all around him. Sudden disorientation made him giddy and anxious until he got his bearings and saw Mack's slumped form at the side of the roof, overlooking the main street. Mack had cleared most of the gathered snow from the roof flooring.

Behind the community hall was a stretch of open land, and around that were rows of houses. All of it indistinct and covered in snow. Either side of the hall were more darkened houses. Another dead village, Seth thought, and tried to push away the sense of despair needling at him.

The snow-flecked wind swept over him, chilling his bones, making his teeth chatter. He wondered how Mack could be up here for so long without freezing. And then the thought came to Seth, of finding Mack rigid, cold and lifeless on the lawn chair where he conducted his watch of the surrounding streets.

Seth looked to the sky and hoped for a glimpse of stars,

but there was nothing except a thick ceiling of snow clouds. He walked towards Mack, and coughed once to announce his presence.

"I knew you were there," Mack said. "Noisy lad."

"Sorry," Seth said, unsure why he was apologising. He stood next to Mack. Beyond the waist-high lip of the roof was the darkened village, desolate and derelict. "Quinn asked me to bring some food up to you. And some whiskey."

In the light of the small camping lantern, Mack looked up at Seth. He was swaddled in thick blankets, with his hood raised over his head so that only his face was exposed to the falling snow and cold air. "About time. Thought I was gonna starve to death up here. Let's have the whiskey."

"Quinn said not to let you drink it all."

"I bet he did. Always acting like the elder brother, he is. Give it." One hand reached out from the mass of blankets, palm up, impatient.

Seth handed the bottle to him. Mack unscrewed the cap, took a deep pull, and burped after he'd finished. He wiped his mouth and placed the bottle beside his chair. Seth gave Mack the food he'd brought: a bowl of swiftly cooling baked beans and meatballs. A plastic fork.

"It's not much," said Seth, pulling on his gloves. "Sorry."

"It's enough," Mack said, forking a meatball into his mouth. He chewed, squinted up at Seth. "We have to be careful with the food."

Seth put his hands in his pockets. "I've been trying not to think about that."

"The food?"

"Yeah. And everything else. Supplies."

"We'll manage. We'll survive."

"Okay." Seth wasn't convinced, but he didn't press Mack further. He folded his arms over his chest, shivering as the gusting wind pushed and pulled at him. "It doesn't feel very safe up here."

"Safe..." Mack said the word like he found it distasteful. "You think everyone's safe down there below? Safe is relative. It's meaningless out here."

"How do you know if the army base is still there...or was ever there at all?"

Mack looked down at the street as he finished his food. He scraped every last morsel and dreg of sauce from inside the bowl. When he was done, he put down the bowl and took another swig from the whiskey. "Pull up a pew and sit down."

Seth grabbed the spare chair from nearby and sat down. Mack handed him the whiskey. He drank a little, and a bit more, then several gulps. The whiskey burned the back of his mouth, but left some pleasing warmth in his chest.

"That's good stuff," said Mack. "Quinn can always be relied on to find decent whiskey. But to answer your question: I have no idea if the army base is still there. None of us have any idea. Not even Quinn knows."

Seth passed the bottle back. "How did you find out about it in the first place?"

"It was on the BBC News, before the power went out. People were told to go there, because there were no other safe places to go. Our farm had already been attacked by some kind of big lizard. Killed all our cows. We drove it away with fire."

"You and Quinn were farmers?"

Mack sighed. "The farm first belonged to our father, but when he died about twenty years ago, it was left to us in his will. Mother had already been dead for a few years."

"You and Quinn, you've done a great thing," said Seth. "You've saved a lot of people."

Mack swigged from the bottle. "No one is saved until we reach the army base."

"If it's still there..."

"I have faith."

"You're religious?"

"Not in *that* way. Not really. But Quinn is. Got all of that from our mother. But he's fairly low key about it. Sometimes I envy him."

"Why's that?"

"Because he believes in something greater. I don't believe in anything much."

Seth noticed that a third of the bottle was already gone. His face was starting to feel numb around his eyes and in his cheeks. "Quinn said not to let you drink the whole bottle."

"I won't," Mack said. "You're drinking it, too."

Seth smiled. "Fair point."

"Don't move, Seth."

"What?"

Mack's voice dipped to a murmur as he looked down at the street. "Don't move. Something's down there."

Seth followed his gaze. At first he couldn't discern what Mack was looking at, but then his eyes adjusted to the darkness. His breath caught in his throat.

It was the figures he'd seen before. Shadowy forms, standing at different points in the street, and whose only definition was the silhouettes of their bodies. They looked to have crooked antlers sprouting from their heads, making them more than eight feet tall. They all looked terribly thin.

"You see them?" Mack said, slowly manoeuvring his rifle below the lip of the roof, ready to bring it into a firing position.

Seth didn't take his eyes from the antlered forms. "I see them."

The men spoke in whispers.

"What the fuck are they?" said Mack.

"I've seen them before."

"When did you see them?"

"On the journey here."

"And you didn't think of telling me or Quinn?"

"I wasn't sure what they were, and they didn't seem like a threat. They were just standing there, like they are now. Just watching."

"Shine your torch down there, Seth."

"What?"

"Shine your fucking torch."

Seth didn't want to see their faces. He was quite sure of that. "I don't want to."

"Don't be a wimp."

"I'm not."

Seth was about to do it, when he heard a light thump behind them. Mack heard it, too, and they both turned around. Seth raised his torch to reveal one of the antlered bipeds. Both men flinched when they saw its face.

"Holy fuck," said Mack. "That's something new."

Seth's legs felt watery and loose. "It's good at climbing."

It was vaguely human, but only in the basic shape of its body. It was emaciated, with shrivelled genitalia, its ashen grey skin dotted with matted hair and pulled tight over its bones. A bestial thing with blackened, twisted antlers, and glowing white eyes within its sunken face. The bones of its nose had collapsed inward. Its drooling mouth was deformed by an abundance of gnarled, jagged teeth. Its hands were long-fingered, tipped with black claws.

"They've been hunting us," said Seth.

Mack put his rifle to his shoulder. "Just like every other fucking monster out there. Fuck 'em all!"

CHAPTER TWENTY-SIX

The beast jerked its head forward, eyes blazing, and growled deep in its throat. Its body twitched and trembled, as if in the throes of some addiction or sickness.

It lunged for the men, snarling and hissing, claws raking at the air.

Mack fired his rifle. The loud report smarted in Seth's ears.

The beast fell back and looked down at the bleeding wound in its stomach. It tottered on gnarled, scabrous legs.

Below them, inside the building, windows shattered. Screams followed.

Mack worked the rifle bolt, ejecting a bullet casing to the floor. Seth kept the torchlight centred upon the creature; it placed its clawed hands at its wounded stomach, then let out a roar that turned his guts to water. He almost dropped the torch from the shaking of his hands.

Then the creature charged again, claws raised, lips peeled back from its awful teeth.

Mack shot the thing in its face, and the back of its skull exploded. The creature toppled backwards, and the roof flooring trembled when it collapsed, limbs twitching, bleeding out until its black heart stopped.

More creatures began rising from the edge of the roof around Seth and Mack, hauling themselves over the lip, growling and snarling.

"Get downstairs!" Mack told Seth. "Help Quinn and the others. I'll hold these fuckers off."

"What?"

Mack chambered another rifle round. "Go, Seth. Do as you're told, lad."

"But..."

"No time. Fuck off."

Seth stumbled away as Mack began firing at the creatures. He opened the roof hatch and fell down the ladder as animalistic howls of pain rang out from the roof.

He ran through the corridor to the doorway at the back of the main room.

The creatures were already inside.

*

Seth slipped on blood in the doorway, and held onto the jamb to stay on his feet. Speechless, he stared at the scene before him. In the flickering light of candles and lanterns, all was chaos and violence. Sobs and screams mixed with the blood-curdling bestial cries of the creatures. A chaotic thrashing of bodies as the monsters attacked. Shattered windows in the light of lanterns. Shards of glass on the floor. The creatures had burst through the windows and smashed down the front door. They were inside the hall. Feeding on people. Other refugees fought back or tried to escape.

Through the panicked crowd, Seth saw Andy, Ruby and Delia standing with their backs against the far wall to his right side. Delia held Jack in her arms as he wailed. She looked terrified. Ruby held a short wooden club of some kind, raising it before her. Andy gripped a carving knife in his right hand, and his eyes were so wide that they could have spilled from their sockets.

Seth started towards them, pushing his way through. He flinched from the bark of Callum's shotgun. He glimpsed Quinn firing his pistol at a shrieking monster that ran at him with stringy viscera clasped in its spindly hands. Brief sights of terrified faces amidst the flailing, struggling bodies and clamouring forms. Pools of blood on the floor.

To his right, in one rear corner of the room, the children cowered in a huddled group, guarded by a few men and women armed with crowbars, knives and hammers. Seth glanced around, shielding his face from jutting elbows and legs; a misdirected hand struck him on the side of the head. Blood splattered upon him from his left side, and someone's cries became a choking gurgle. A scream filled his ears, pulsed inside his skull. Near-witless, he looked down at a severed leg detached just below the knee on the floor. Entrails and offal. A ravaged body, made androgynous by the violence acted upon it. Everything manic and hysterical.

A man staggered past clutching his opened stomach, trying to keep his guts from slopping past his red hands. And while stumbling through the scrum of bodies and violence, suffering glancing blows from those around him, Seth saw Callum dump his shotgun and pull out a knife.

The creatures grabbed Callum, slashed and clawed at him. His hat dropped to the floor, and his greasy hair spilled down. He spat and swore, fighting with all his strength until he was lost to a feeding frenzy of horribly thin bodies and swiping claws. Blackened mouths gnawed and snapped. Hot arterial blood spurted on the floor and walls as he was quickly dismantled.

Other people were dragged away screaming, to be slaughtered in the shadows at the front of the hall.

Seth had almost reached Andy, Delia and Jack, when a stray elbow caught him in the face. His vision spun, dotted with black motes, as he fell, clutching his nose. His breathing was ragged. The floor was wet. He looked up to see a man holding a Molotov cocktail, preparing to throw it towards the front of the hall. He had just arched his arm back when one of the horned creatures bolted past him and clawed at his face - and he dropped the petrol bomb with a high-pitched wail.

The second before the petrol bomb hit the floor seemed to last forever. The bottle shattered, the burning wick igniting the petrol, and flames blossomed on the floor.

The man was set alight, the fire surging up his legs and then over the rest of him. The flames spread to the nearest wall, setting alight curtains and billowing grey smoke, which began to slowly fill the room. He coughed and spat. His eyes were stinging.

"Get out!" Quinn ordered to those still alive. "All of you. Get out!"

The survivors were already fleeing towards the back door. Seth glimpsed Andy leading Delia and Jack away from the flames. Within the smoke Seth was kicked and struck in the panicked rush. Survivors were clutching supplies, provisions, blankets, and even each other, as they evacuated.

Battered, bruised, and weakened from the smoke, Seth struggled out on all fours. The creatures roared from nearby. He hoped that most people had escaped from the building.

The flames grew higher and spread.

He was on his knees, gathering the strength to stand, when a scabrous hand grabbed his left foot and pulled him down onto his stomach, slamming his ribs against the floor. The air was knocked from his chest. He glanced back and saw that the creature could only use its free hand to drag itself along; its legs were broken and useless. The creature snarled as spit frothed from its blackened lips, eyes blazing coldly.

Seth managed to flip onto his back, and tried to kick the creature's hand away, but it held on tight, squeezing with immense strength the ankle bones under his skin.

He cried out.

The creature opened its mouth to bite at his legs. Serrated teeth dripped in the light of the fire.

Seth's hand fell upon a hatchet. With all the strength he could muster, he sat up in one quick movement and buried the hatchet in the top of its skull, right between its gnarled antlers. He let out a cry borne of mania and anger, then let go of the hatchet as the monster released his foot. It slumped raggedly before him, gasping a final breath from its horrid mouth.

Seth staggered to his feet as the fire spread, flames licking at the ceiling and consuming the walls to each side. He shielded his face from the heat, wincing, eyes streaming and aching. The room blurred in the swarming smoke. His mouth and throat were dry and sore, and his skin prickled in the heated air. He had to move.

The revving and spluttering of the tractor's engine rose above the roaring of the flames, and then began to fade, moving away.

He fled, the fire reaching for his heels, the walls collapsing behind him.

*

Seth escaped the community hall moments before the roof collapsed. He stumbled clear of the burning building and fell down in the snow, wretched and beyond exhaustion.

He looked around, but there was no sign of the creatures, and the tractor and the refugees were nowhere to be seen. His relief at their escape was tempered by the realisation that he was completely vulnerable. Panic and fear worked inside his stomach. A sense of loneliness and desolation came to him, and all he wanted to do was lie down and go to sleep.

The fire raged thirty yards behind him, flames reaching to the dark sky. Implosions and dull crackling from within. The street was aglow from the inferno and, from its light, shadows writhed against the outer walls of houses. He felt used up and utterly forlorn. His clothes were singed, as were his eyebrows. He pawed the snow over the tender skin of his face and into his mouth, and it tasted of nothingness.

A sound behind him made him drop the snow from his hands. He wiped his mouth. He listened, not daring to move at first. Something there, that had been barely audible above the noise of the fire. He patted his pockets for anything to use as a weapon, but there was nothing, and he didn't think he had the energy to make a run for it.

He rose and turned around, ready to face his death.

Mack stood before him, a machete in one hand and the whiskey bottle in the other. He was tattered and slumped but he seemed to have escaped without serious injury.

Sudden relief flooded Seth. "I thought you were dead."

Mack snorted, shaking his head despairingly. "I certainly feel like it, lad."

CHAPTER TWENTY-SEVEN

They watched for monsters and retreated to a house down the street from the burning community hall. It was a pyre in the night. The front door of the house was unlocked and the interior was empty of bodies except for a dead hamster in its cage. It was beginning to smell, so Mack buried it in the snow outside.

They sat next to each other on the sofa, wrapped in scavenged blankets. Mack drank whiskey and muttered to himself. They wouldn't be able to put up much of a fight if the antlered creatures attacked again. The room was cold and dark.

"Do you think the fire will spread?" Seth asked. He felt wretched and sick. His ears still throbbed from the gunfire.

Mack swigged from his bottle and grimaced. "It always does."

Seth wasn't sure what that meant, so he said nothing and closed his eyes.

Neither of them slept that night.

First light arrived in grey shades. They swapped their tattered coats for better ones from the house. Mack found two thick woollen hats, both seemingly brand new, and gave one to Seth, who packed some food, a bottle of water, a torch with spare batteries, blankets, and three road flares into a rucksack. Then Mack used a penknife to sharpen one end of a broom handle, whittling it down to a fine point. He figured it would do as a makeshift spear. He handed the improvised weapon to Seth, who smiled tightly.

"Better than nothing," Mack said.

"What do you think happened to the people who lived here?" Seth asked, weighing the weapon in his hands doubtfully. "You think they fled?"

"Maybe," said Mack. "But would they have left this stuff here? Surely they would have taken it with them. It doesn't matter."

Seth supposed it didn't really.

They left the house. The community hall was still burning, and the fire had spread to the adjacent buildings. Smoke streamed upwards in dark plumes. The air smelled of ash.

No snow fell from the sky. Both men looked upwards, surprised.

"Maybe the snow has stopped for good," said Seth.

Mack trudged onwards. "Or it could just be a lull in the storm."

Up the road, following the tracks from the tractor tyres, they stopped and stood over the charred corpse of an antlered creature. It was all twisted and broken in the snow. Bullet wounds in its torso.

Mack spat on it, then turned and walked away. Seth followed, clutching his spear in one hand, the rucksack swinging over his shoulder.

"Carry your rucksack properly," said Mack, glancing back at Seth. "Hook it over both shoulders and behind you; carrying it by one strap will hurt your shoulder eventually."

Seth considered arguing the point, then nodded and did as he was told.

They left the burning village behind.

*

They walked for over an hour, until eventually the tyre tracks led back to the motorway and then northwards. They walked for most of the day, Mack urging Seth on when he faltered.

It was a relief to not encounter any monsters that day. And when Seth could go no farther, Mack finally relented. They settled down for the night in the back of a transit van at the roadside and took turns to check the snowfall, worried that the tractor's tyre tracks would be covered while they rested.

"How many died back at the community hall?" Seth asked. "How many got out alive?" He had tried counting in his head, but his thoughts were muddled. He sat across from Mack, both of them wrapped in blankets against the cold. His teeth ached and chattered.

"I didn't see much," said Mack. His face looked wizened and sickly in the glow of the torchlight.

"Callum died," Seth said. "I saw it happen."

Mack looked at the machete in his hand, resting on his lap. "Did the children make it out? Did Delia and Jack escape?"

"Delia and Jack escaped, but a lot of the children were taken. Quinn is still alive, I'm sure of it."

Mack nodded, gave a fragile smile. "Quinn's a survivor. That's why he's in charge. He'll get the rest of them to safety, eventually, I know he will."

"Is he much older than you?"

"Only three years. Used to give me a lot of shit when we were children, but nothing too bad. Always looked after me at school. Even stopped our father from hitting me once during an argument. My father never tried again."

"What was the argument about?" Seth asked.

"I forget now. Nothing important. But old Dad had a temper. He loved us, though. And he loved our mum." Mack sighed. "That's all gone, now. It's weird looking back at the past, isn't it? I can't stop thinking about the old Clint Eastwood films we used to watch on Sunday afternoons."

Seth sipped some water. "I try not to do it any more. It just makes things worse."

"I'm sorry about your parents."

"It's done now. Like you said, it's all gone."

Mack rested the back of his head against the side of the van. Neither of them spoke for a while. The wind made low sounds as it swept across the snow-covered motorway.

"I think this is it," Mack said, finally. "Properly it." He scratched at his face. There was a faraway look in his eyes.

"What do you mean?" said Seth.

"The end of it all." said Mack. "If we survive, as a species, the ones left alive are going to be in for a terrible time."

"Even worse than now?"

"We're the bottom of the food chain, lad. We're food for the beasts. And if the snow *has* covered the entire planet, it'll be impossible to grow crops or farm livestock. Think about it: Permafrost. An Ice Age. No food except what we can forage from tins and cans. Or hunt. Then there's the problem of finding suitable shelter from the snow and the cold. And, of course, there are the monsters." He sighed, shaking his head slowly as he wiped dirt from his blade.

Seth looked at him, but didn't know what to say.

Mack laid the machete on the floor of the van. "We've just got to keep trying. That's all we can do."

CHAPTER TWENTY-EIGHT

The night passed without incident and it didn't snow in the hours before the grey dawn. When they climbed out of the van, the sky was nothing but a ceiling of white cloud stretching away in every direction. The cold fog had closed in during the night and reduced visibility down to less than twenty yards.

Seth and Mack stood beside the van. There was only silence beyond them. No tracks in the snow, except for the tractor's and their own boot prints. There'd been no visitors in the night.

"Ready to go?" Mack asked.

Seth took a swig from the water bottle. "Yeah."

"How you feeling this morning?"

"Like shit," Seth replied. And he did. It wasn't an exaggeration. Every part of him ached, and his chest was tight. His legs were fighting off cramps and little pains jabbed at his shins. His joints felt stiff and brittle.

"Gotta keep going," said Mack.

"I know. I know."

They kept following the tractor's trail, walking for over two hours before they took a rest and shared a granola bar.

A mile later, they halted when a flock of oversized black moths took to the air from the snow drifts they'd been perched upon. There were half a dozen of them, each measuring a good six feet from the tips of their antennae to the end of their thoraxes. Their wings were coloured with skeins of vivid red.

Mack raised his machete, but Seth placed his hand on the man's arm and shook his head.

"Wait," Seth said. "They're not a threat."

"How do you know?"

They stood there and watched the black moths flutter their wings and swoop through the air above, diving in and out of the white fog like silent wraiths. The only sound Seth could hear was his own heartbeat. He had thought all grace and beauty gone from the world since the snow fell, but now he was transfixed, utterly beholden to the dance of the black moths in the air.

The men were so mesmerised by the moths' display, they didn't notice the giant haggard shape of the vulture-thing until it snatched a moth into its curved claws. The rest of the flock scattered, and Seth and Mack reeled away, stumbling back as it took its prey to ground. It issued a wheezing shriek from its blackened beak. It was yellow-eyed and featherless, save for a few downy scraps. Its wings were papery and thin, spanning more than twenty feet combined. A nightmare vision, pale and shabby.

Seth and Mack hid behind an overturned car and peered out at the thing as it began ripping at the moth's thorax with its busy beak. The moth twitched occasionally, but it had been dead by the time it hit the ground. Its black blood stained the snow.

Within minutes the vulture-thing had dismantled and devoured the moth until all that remained were shredded wings. Then it lifted up from the ground and vanished into the sky with a gurgling cry.

"Christ," said Mack, slumping in the snow. He was shaking his head, gripping the machete with both hands.

Seth looked around for any sign of the flock, but it was gone, fled to some sort of safety.

*

Half a mile later they found the wrecked remains of the tractor and trailer lying across the road.

The snow was stained red.

CHAPTER TWENTY-NINE

"Oh fuck," said Seth, blinking flakes of snow from his eyes.

The tractor was disconnected from the trailer, both lying on their sides and skewed across the northward side of the motorway. There were splatters and pools of frozen blood around the wrecks. Severed body parts and wet-red bones. Smashed supplies and broken boxes of food had been scattered across the road.

Seth and Mack stood crestfallen and shivering. All over the crash site were muddled prints from footwear mixed with smears and smudges. And there were larger tracks, from some kind of creature; something large and heavy, judging by the spaces between the deep indentations of clawed footprints in the snow. Something no smaller than a bull elephant, that moved on four legs. It could have been any kind of nightmare thing.

Seth looked at Mack, who was staring at the tractor cab; the windscreen was mostly gone. Snow was already beginning to shroud the wreckage.

"It happened hours ago," said Mack.

"What do you think did it?" Seth asked.

Mack shrugged, his face terribly pale, and he began searching the crash site. Seth helped him.

"Do you recognise any of the remains?" said Seth. He felt sick just from asking the question. If he found baby Jack's cold corpse amongst the wreckage, it would be too much for him. He was already close to tears, and it felt as if any hope that remained had seeped away to be replaced by a creeping dread that filled his stomach. He remembered the train crash and the bodies of the passengers in the snow.

The world was full of death.

"There's not much to recognise," said Mack. And he was right; a few arms, a leg, some tangled entrails and anonymous lumps of flesh.

There was no sign of Quinn, Delia, Andy, Ruby or baby Jack.

The snow fell in the dreadful silence. The white fog moved in. The end of the world had arrived with the cold.

*

Dusk closed in with faint shrieks from across the land. Echoing cries of terrible creatures and monstrosities.

Seth and Mack huddled beneath the overhanging trailer through the night hours, taking turns to sleep and keeping watch in the darkness.

CHAPTER THIRTY

"What do we do now?" Seth asked. It was morning. The snow seemed like drifts of ash in the grey dawn light.

"Keep heading north," Mack told him, checking the compass he'd pulled from his pocket. "It's all we can do."

"Do you think any of them got away?"

"I don't know. I hope so." Mack's throat worked as he stared at the machete in his hand.

Seth looked to the ground. A fresh snowfall had covered any tracks they might follow. He slumped, buried his hands in his coat pockets, and tried to suppress the cold futility that curdled his stomach and made his legs heavy. He felt exhausted and he couldn't stop shuddering in his clothes. Parts of him were numb. He envisaged his toes blackening, flesh sloughing away to reveal bone. The cold was claiming him one piece at a time. When he considered the distance ahead and the monsters waiting for them, it was all he could not to collapse in the snow and sob like a child.

"Let's go," Mack said.

They moved on.

*

An hour later they sighted a service station area beyond the side of the motorway, and followed the slip road towards it, hoping to find survivors from their group. The building would be adequate shelter for anyone who'd escaped the crash site.

Both sides of the access road to the service station were lined with conifers; the trees were burdened with heavy snow upon their branches, wilting under the strain. The road led Seth and Mack to a car park, beyond which stood the service station itself, which was basically a mall-type building, with several different shops, fast food outlets, and facilities inside. Seth had been here before, a few years ago, when he and his parents had driven up north for a holiday in the Lake District.

Mack started across the broad expanse of snowed-under tarmac. Seth followed. They passed abandoned cars and lumpen shapes under the snow that might have been corpses.

They arrived at the short flight of stone steps leading to the front entrance. Mack halted, Seth beside him. Beyond the glass doors was impenetrable darkness.

Seth took out his torch. He wiped snow from his face and winced inside his hood. "Do you really think anyone's in there?"

Mack sniffed, glanced around, before looking at the entrance. His jaw tensed. "Let's find out."

*

They went inside and stood beside each other in the vestibule, a row of standing ATMs to one side of them. Seth's torchlight swept the way ahead.

"I don't think anyone's here," said Seth, keeping his voice low. He ground his teeth.

"We'll just have a look around," Mack replied.

"Fair enough."

They entered the main area - a wide walkway lined by shops, coffee houses and various fast food outlets. All of them were dark and silent. Deserted. Seth directed the torch towards the open seating area of a Burger King, moving the light over abandoned meals on tables and toppled chairs. His stomach crumpled at the sight of decaying food. A few jackets and coats were left hanging over the backs of some of the chairs.

"Stop," said Mack.

Seth did so, but frowned at Mack. "What?"

"We're not alone." Mack pointed at one shopfront to their right. Seth shone the torchlight through the plate glass and into the shadows. His heart stuttered as he saw the slumped figures inside several shops on both sides of the walkway; one was sitting with its head bowed at a table near the back of a Starbuck's, far enough from the torchlight to be ambiguous - as were the others. They could have been mannequins but for their twitching movements as they turned away from the searching torchlight. Most were hunched over, stooped and solemn, like old shades of consumers who'd passed through on their way to distant destinations.

"You see 'em?" said Mack.

Seth was about to step towards the nearest shopfront, but then thought better of it. He squinted, wiped his mouth. "Yeah, I see."

"I don't like the look of them."

"What if they're people from Quinn's group?" Seth almost asked if Quinn was among them, until he noticed the apprehension on Mack's pallid face.

Mack stared into the shadows. His mouth opened, quivered a little. His voice was the meekest Seth had heard it since they'd met. "I don't think so, lad. I don't think so."

They walked on.

Directly ahead of them, the torchlight found the motionless figure of a woman standing in their way. They stopped ten yards from her. Mack swore under his breath. The torchlight threw the woman's spindly shadow upon the floor, revealing her twisted and misshapen body. Lumpen shapes bulged beneath her hooded coat, and her face was pinkish, shining with something like sweat. Her eyes were stretched wide and reddened with burst capillaries. She muttered through a crumpled mouth. She held a small pickaxe in the hand that wasn't swollen purple and fit to burst with infection. Seth only realised the bulging of her stomach when it juddered violently, as if manipulated from within.

"What the fuck?" Seth said. He kept the torchlight upon the woman, who didn't shy away or even blink.

Mack raised his machete.

The woman wheezed, her blackened teeth chattering, as her swollen hand undid her coat down the middle to reveal her full glory. She arched back her head and cried out in pain. She was naked beneath the coat, and her entire torso was infested with red tumours, inside which some kind of black insectoid larvae squirmed and coiled. Parasites within membranes. She twitched and shuddered with their movement.

She looked at Seth and Mack and smiled dreamily. Then she raised the pickaxe above her head and staggered towards them on tottering legs.

They reeled away as the axe swung down and clanged upon the hard floor. The woman shrieked, lifted the axe again, and jerked her head around to locate the men as they backed away. Within the hood of the coat, her face was sagging from her skull.

Seth stood back against the plate glass of a shop window. The torchlight swayed around. Mack lit a flare, lunged forwards and jabbed it towards the woman's head, but she dodged him and swung the axe horizontally, narrowly missing his chest. She stumbled. Mack raised his machete before she could regain her balance and sliced a deep cut across her swollen forearm. The woman stepped back, holding the wounded arm close to her side, blood and pus pattering onto the floor.

Mack retreated two steps, waiting for her to attack again, when the woman made a low gurgling sound and dropped the axe. Her entire body fell to violent trembling and she collapsed to her knees, gazing down at her stomach as the larvae burst out, chittering and writhing. She laughed, and it was one of the most insane sounds Seth had ever heard.

Mack slashed her throat, and she fell down with the newborn worms squirming beneath her.

Mack grabbed Seth and pulled him along.

Then they stopped. Looked around at the large windows of the shopfronts.

"Christ," said Seth.

The other people had come to look at them. They were naked, hand-in-hand behind the plate glass. And the black larvae infesting their stomachs slowly awakened.

CHAPTER THIRTY-ONE

Seth and Mack stumbled through the back exit of the service station and into the falling snow outside. They didn't stop until the building vanished into the distance behind them, and then they collapsed to the ground, panting and wheezing. Those people, Seth thought, left behind in some sort of hell, hosts for the black larvae.

"I didn't see Quinn," Mack whispered. "He wasn't there. None of our people were there."

"I know," said Seth.

Mack sat in the snow, head lowered to his chest. The machete lay by his feet, gleaming with the dull light. His voice was barely audible when he spoke. "It's fucked, Seth. It's all fucked. What sort of world is this now? All those people back there...incubators for whatever those things were. It just gets worse and worse."

Seth crouched beside him, shivering in the cold. "We have to keep moving north, like you said before. We can't stop."

Mack looked at Seth. The machete was in his hand again. "How many people have you seen die?"

"What?"

"How many people?"

"I don't know."

"You'd know if you thought about it. But you don't want to think about it. I don't blame you, lad. It's too much; it's all too fucking much."

They stood, dusted the snow from themselves, and moved on, hunched and staggering as the north wind bore down on them.

*

An hour later, a sign at the side of the motorway slowly coalesced out of the falling snow. Seth and Mack halted, tired and sagging like drunkards. The sky howled. Mack checked the compass in his hand.

According to the sign, the army base was two miles away, so they took the narrow exit road from the motorway and headed into country roads and weaving tracks. They walked in silence, waiting to reach the end, slogging over the snow, watching for signs of their people.

Seth shook his head to clear his vision, and wiped bits of snow from around his eyes. The pain in his legs was just below tolerable, but the cold numbed his gloved hands and slowed his thoughts. He lagged behind Mack on the exposed roads amidst the white hills. The falling snow dwindled to a drizzle of grey flakes.

In the adjacent field to the right of the road, a dead beast lay fallen. They stopped to stare at it, this broken titan. It was some kind of arachnid thing. Its corpse spanned almost the length of the field, its legs were splayed and crumpled, and as long as telephone poles. Black blood stained the snow. The bulbous mass of its central body had been torn and ransacked, spilling fluids and insides.

Mack snorted. "Just imagine the thing that killed *this* thing."

Seth dragged his eyes from the carcass to glance about. "How far to the army base? Please tell me it's nearby. There can't be much further to go."

"Less than a mile. Somewhere around here."

"I'd kill for a cheeseburger."

"I don't think they'll be serving those at the base."

"I'd take the thinnest, most pathetic, burger going. I don't care."

"A decent steak wouldn't go amiss," said Mack. "And chips."

"And onion rings?"

"Definitely."

Seth almost laughed. His stomach clenched with cravings for cooked meat and carbs. Saliva gathered at the back of his mouth and sluiced over his molars. The phantom taste of salty McDonald's fries, summoned up by some half-buried memory, made his chest ache with a maddening pang.

"Come on," said Mack. "Let's find that fucking base."

CHAPTER THIRTY-TWO

"Oh God," said Mack. "Christ Almighty."

They'd slipped through the broken front gates to stand on the tarmac track that led towards the heart of the base. The wind had died to a murmur during a lull in the falling snow. Everything was beset by a lifeless silence.

Seth and Mack walked amongst the ruins within the demolished perimeter fence.

Something terrible had visited the base and brought devastation and death. The buildings were smashed to pieces, leaving only a few disparate walls standing amidst toppled masonry and fields of debris, fallen wooden beams and lengths of splintered timber. There were great gouges in the ground, carved by monstrous strength and rage.

They searched through the remains. There were no bodies, just the occasional lump of frozen, unidentifiable flesh. Meat detritus and bone trash.

Seth prodded with his foot a fist-sized piece of rubble. He looked over at Mack, who stood motionless near the burned-out barracks and stared out towards the far side of the perimeter where part of the fence still remained standing.

Picking his way through the wreckage, Seth walked over to Mack. They regarded each other for a moment, Seth's dismay and numb horror reflecting back from Mack's eyes, which were reddened and miserable. Seth had to look away.

Faraway booms that could have been monsters or

quakes within the earth, rose and reverberated, then faded into the distance.

"So, that's it, isn't it?" said Mack. "The end of it all."

Seth stared off into the white fog beyond them, a part of him hoping that some immense terror would emerge to finally claim them, release them from this state of purgatory.

"I don't know," he answered.

Mack glanced around. "I reckon the attack happened no more than two days ago."

Seth rubbed at his face, one hand grazing over his darkening stubble. His skin felt blotchy and dried out under his fingers. His forehead felt like it'd been scoured by sandpaper. The compulsion to lie down in the ruins and accept his fate was suddenly all he could think about; it was an itch inside his head. Tears brimmed in his eyes. He thought of Andy, Ruby, Delia and Jack. He bowed his head.

"What do we do now? We have nowhere to go."

"We'll have to stay here tonight," Mack replied, not taking his gaze from the surrounding white fog. "There's nothing else to be done."

*

Mack found a metal hatch in the ground, but despite both of them working at it, trying to pull it open, it didn't budge or even shift on its hinges. The hatch was approximately the size of a manhole cover, but square and made of thick steel.

They gave up after twenty minutes, both of them slumping to the ground with aching arms and hands.

Mustering the last of their energy, they scavenged for supplies in the ruins, and found enough to construct a makeshift refuge in one corner of the half-collapsed husk of an outbuilding. The roof was gone, so they hung sheets and lengths of ragged tarpaulin as shelter against the elements, pinning and fixing them with pieces of timber and metal poles. It would hold for the night.

Mack built a small campfire and kept the flames low.

They sat inside the shabby den they'd made, wrapped in their blankets, drinking water and eating crisps. The wind picked up, wailing as darkness fell with flurries of snow, and soon the night was upon them with all its swarming shadows.

*

When Seth woke in the dark, the fire had burned out and Mack was missing from the shelter. Panicked, he pawed about for his torch and finally found it buried under the blankets Mack had apparently cast aside. Then he grabbed the axe.

He switched on the torch and clambered from the shelter. The snow fell against his face. He gritted his teeth, breathed hard through his nose, then swept the torchlight around the surrounding wreckage and toppled walls.

There was no sign of Mack at all.

When Seth emerged outside, the wind pulled at him and filled his ears with its white noise. It stole his breath and stung his eyes, made it hard to think or gather his bearings. He gulped, swallowed, grimaced in the blizzard. The darkness was all about him, suffocating and dense, working at his nerves and thickening his fear. For a moment he felt like the last person in the world. This made him think about his chances of survival on his own, and if he was capable of survival on his own. And then he wondered if his life was, in fact, even worth saving. His inconsequential existence. His worthless life. He could be the last person left alive and be utterly ignorant of it.

He wanted to scream.

*

A red flare ignited ahead of Seth. Mack was standing in the snow not far beyond the destroyed buildings of the base. He raised the flare above his head as he looked out at the night. Like he was signalling for something, Seth thought. The flare spat and sizzled.

Seth shouted to the man, but the screaming wind and falling snow muffled his voice to a useless murmur. With one hand to his face, he trudged towards Mack, moving past snow-shrouded debris and jutting metal beams, weaving through the destruction. Floundering like a man in the throes of an illness. He called out, his throat scratchy and dry, the axe wavering in his hand.

Mack turned around when Seth got within fifteen yards of him. His face was impassive within the frame of the coat hood, his mouth a straight line. In the burning of the flare, he looked older than before, somehow. Something was wrong with his eyes; they were too pale and his pupils had shrunk to black pinpricks.

He told Seth to stay back.

Seth halted, confused and bleary-eyed, shivering as the wind lashed against him. "What's wrong, Mack? What're you doing?"

"Something is here with us. Nearby."

"A monster?"

Mack glanced over his shoulder at the darkness behind him, and then returned his gaze to Seth. "We can't let this be the end of everything."

Seth had opened his mouth to reply when a shattering roar boomed out of the darkness. He flinched and stepped back, almost tripping on a piece of debris. Then he froze, looking at Mack, who merely bowed his head slightly and turned towards the giant shape.

The ground trembled all around them. And, with the sound of the front gates being swept aside, the monstrous thing took form. It was as tall as a seven-storey block of flats and just as wide, teeming with bioluminescent lights that writhed upon its dark bulk. It bellowed and barked throatily, utterly alien and terrifying. The titan's massive lungs took inhalations with deep, tremulous bursts. The air around it seemed to quiver.

Seth dropped to a crouch and peered out from behind a pile of debris. Slack-mouthed, he gawped in silence, trembling like a scared child. His bones felt like brittle sticks.

Mack shouted up at the monster, goading it, shaking the flare in his hand. He stood ready, waiting, in acceptance.

Black tendrils shot down from the entity's bulk and seized Mack by his arms. He dropped the flare, and it lay in the snow, spitting out its glowing red spray. He cried out something Seth couldn't hear over the keening wind, and was snatched away, into darkness.

Seth was near-witless, beyond terrified, and he fled to their shelter where he hid in a nest of blankets and old sheets, crying and whimpering.

The monster roared, shaking the remains of the base and its foundations.

Seth clasped his hands over his mouth and tried not to scream as the world slipped away.

*

He woke shuddering and panicked into a half-light between worlds. That familiar deathly silence.

A tall figure stood over him in the collapsed wreck of the shelter, while wind rattled about the ruins. The figure shone a torch at his face. The storm had died, but the snow still fell steadily.

"Mack?" Seth managed to mutter through his dry mouth and chattering teeth. The pain in his head had him worried that his skull was splitting open. He thought about the god-monster, the thing that had taken Mack, and suppressed the urge to cry.

The figure crouched, directed the torchlight away from Seth's face. It wasn't Mack. The figure wore a black balaclava and army fatigues. An automatic rifle hung over one shoulder.

Two other armed figures were standing several yards away, watching him.

"Help," Seth wheezed. "Please help me. There's no one else left."

"It's going to be all right," the man said. His voice was harsh, but not unkind. "There's shelter for you here. Come with us."

CHAPTER THIRTY-THREE

Seth came out of a deep, dreamless sleep in a bed within a darkened room. Silence, except for his panicked breathing and the grinding of his heart. He looked around, dislocated and floppy-limbed, as he sat up, the bedsheets falling away from his chest. His head swam and most parts of him ached and burned with muscle fatigue. The cold air prickled his face and forearms. He cleared his throat and coughed up a yellowish lump of phlegm.

The bare lightbulb overhead gave detail to his surroundings. The walls, ceiling and floor were grey and bare, like a cell, and that troubled him. A black door on the other side of the room. No windows. The faint smell of bleach.

He wore a t-shirt and boxer shorts that weren't his own. The implication that someone had undressed him and seen his naked body made him feel strangely ashamed. He swivelled and sat on the edge of the bed, his movements sluggish and poorly-coordinated.

The room swayed when he stood, and he breathed slowly, rubbing his eyes. The floor was cold. When he took his hands from his face, he stepped slowly to the door and tried the handle. It was locked. He shook it in both hands, then stood back, shaking his head. He was about to start banging his fists on the door when the lock clicked and the door opened. He backed away, hands half-raised, tense and anxious. One hand formed a fist.

Andy entered the room, closely followed by a man in a

dull white lab coat. Seth suddenly wondered if everything before had been a dream of madness and this place was a refuge for the insane. He stepped away, glancing back and forth between the men.

"Seth," Andy said. "You're awake, at last."

Ruby walked in with an armful of clothes, and gave a wan smile. "How are you feeling?"

Seth rubbed his face. "What's going on? Where am I?"

"Everything's fine," said Andy. "You can relax, man."

"I thought all of you were dead," said Seth.

Andy glanced at Ruby. "We made it. Not all of us. But we made it." He indicated the clothes and boots to Seth. "These should be the right sizes for you."

Seth took them from Ruby. He stepped back again, holding the pile in front of his body and thanked them all.

The man in the lab coat was waxen-faced and painfully thin. He blinked, pursed his flat mouth, which was framed by an untidy goatee beard, then leaned forward, appraising Seth with bloodshot eyes. His hair hadn't seen a brush in a while, and his clothes hung loosely upon him. He dropped his hands into the pockets of his lab coat.

"Hello, Seth, I'm Doctor Felton. I hope this isn't too much of a shock. How are you feeling?"

"A bit rough. Bit blurry around the edges."

Andy offered Seth a sympathetic smile with something like relief in his eyes.

"That's not surprising," said Felton. "You were in quite a state when you were found."

"How long have I been here?"

"Two days."

"I've been unconscious for two days?"

"More or less," said Andy. "You woke up yesterday for a short while, muttering about random stuff."

"Where am I?"

"You're in the bunker," Felton said.

*

Seth dressed in the clothes Ruby had given to him. A thick jumper and jeans, plus a pair of frayed socks, all of it creased but clean. He pulled on the boots, which were a little tight around the toes but comfortable enough for him. The clothes had seen previous owners, but he was just glad to be warm, despite the niggling thought that he was wearing a dead man's ensemble. Warm at last.

Felton gave him a small bottle of water, and he downed half of it in one go. Then Andy and Ruby hugged Seth, bringing him close to tears.

Now they walked a narrow corridor, which to Seth appeared exactly the same as the first corridor they'd gone through. Felton limped beside him, with Andy and Ruby following close behind, hand-in-hand. Seth was pleased for his new friends. In the cramped confines, Seth could smell his own body odour, sour and musky. There were no windows and the grey walls radiated cold. Grainy dust and grit crackled under their shoes. Intermittent bare lightbulbs hung from the concrete ceiling and grew pitch black shadows from the men.

"You've got electricity," said Seth. "Impressive."

Felton nodded. "That's not all. We've got an underground reservoir that provides drinking water, and a waste treatment plant. You can even have a shower later. The air temperature is kept at around fifteen degrees. The power generators are fed by fuel tanks stored deeper into the complex. They'll keep us going."

"For how long?" asked Seth.

"I'm not allowed to tell you that."

"Oh."

"Don't worry; it'll be a long time before we run out of our original supply."

"Okay."

"The bunker is beneath the base, or what remains of it. Seventy feet below the ground, made of reinforced concrete and steel. It's equipped to hold over five hundred people. Most of the complex isn't even being used, and those parts are left without power. Saves fuel."

Seth recalled the three men who'd found him after Mack's death. "Are there soldiers here?"

"The ones who survived," said Felton. "The bunker is much too big for the number of people down here. It's a bloody tragedy. We could have saved more civilians. Although I suppose it's better to have too much space than not enough."

"How many people are here?"

Felton cleared his throat, wiped his mouth, and then returned the hand back to its pocket. "Forty-seven civilians, yourself included. Then there's me, the only doctor on site. Eight soldiers."

Seth did the maths in his head. "Fifty-six people in total. Jesus." His voice was sombre. He felt sick. It was a paltry number. Pathetic. It was the brink of extinction.

"We could do with Jesus," Felton said. "He'd be a great help with our food supplies."

"Quinn died," Andy said from behind them. "It happened when the tractor crashed. We were attacked by some big bastard thing."

"We found the crash site," said Seth. He paused, swallowed. "Mack's dead too."

"I know."

"What about Delia and Jack?"

"They made it. They're fine."

It was a miracle of a sort, and he held on to it with all he had.

Ruby cleared her throat. "After the attack, those of us still alive walked the rest of the way to the base. We lost a few more people on the way. Andy led us, like Moses guiding his people out of the desert. Then the soldiers found us and let us into the bunker."

A dismal look passed over Felton's pale face. "The death toll must be catastrophic. It's hard to believe, really."

Seth was about to ask the doctor if he meant the death toll for the world or just the UK, when the corridor widened and they arrived at a set of double-doors.

They halted.

"This is Medical," said Felton. "Time for your check up, Seth. Follow me."

CHAPTER THIRTY-FOUR

The medical bay was a large room, approximately two thousand square feet in size, with a white ceiling and white walls. Strip lighting buzzed and glowed. Blue linoleum covered the floor. Ten beds lined part of the wall on one side of the room. Five of the beds were occupied by patients, four of whom were asleep. The only one currently awake was staring up at the ceiling. One side of his face was heavily bandaged. The other patients looked in worse shape, with legs or arms encased in plaster casts. One of them muttered in her sleep. A female nurse sat nearby at a desk, studying a textbook while she sipped black coffee. She glanced up at Felton's group and nodded.

"I'm quite busy at the moment," said Felton. "Aside from the usual colds and sprained ankles, there have been a few serious injuries. Had some problems with infection from untreated wounds and such. And then there's the psychological issues. We could do with a mental health specialist, as most people are still in shock." He gestured to large wall cabinets on the left side of the room. "Fortunately, we're pretty well stocked as far as medication goes. At the moment. There's a separate ward adjacent to this room, but it's not in use. We've also got a few smaller, single rooms, like the one you stayed in. You wouldn't believe the amount of paracetamol and ibuprofen some people go through; we're always looking to stock up on those items. Asthma medication, too. Fortunately we've got loads of cod liver oil tablets..."

They walked past assorted medical equipment that Seth

vaguely recognised from hospital visits. Bulky electronics and snaking wires. A defibrillator on a chrome worktop. Shelves crammed with textbooks and thick medical volumes. The air smelled of bleach and coffee.

Felton stopped by a workstation. He told Seth to take off his jumper and t-shirt and sit on the edge of one of the beds, so he could be examined. Andy and Ruby stood several yards away, whispering to each other, exchanging brief smiles.

"We'll come back after Doctor Felton's finished with you, Seth," Ruby said. She and Andy left the room.

"Young love," Felton observed.

"Good for them," replied Seth.

"Indeed. You can have a shower after we're done."

"Do I smell that bad?"

Felton coughed out a dry laugh. "A little bit. No offence."

"None taken."

Felton talked through Seth's medical background, checking for pre-existing conditions, and then he gave him a swift but thorough physical examination. Half an hour later, he was done. The doctor gave him the all-clear. He was in pretty good condition apart from a few muscle strains, bruised limbs, and some patches of sore skin on his face, all of which were easily treatable.

Seth put his clothes back on. He craved some decent food. Maybe a beer, if there was one around. God, yes!

Moments later, a soldier wearing creased fatigues entered the medical bay. He was bull-necked, stocky, with a shaven head. The rolled-up sleeves of his fatigues exposed tattoos on his forearms.

"Sergeant Hanso," Felton said. "Good to see you."

"Is he ready?" the sergeant asked, glancing at Seth.

"Yes, we've just finished. He's all yours."

"What's going on?" Seth asked.

The sergeant's face remained impassive, and this time he looked straight at Seth. "We're off to see the captain. He has some questions for you."

*

Seth recognised Hanso's voice. He was the soldier who'd first found him in the ruins of the army base above. The walk to Captain Miller's office was done in silence; they passed only a few other people, civilian survivors running errands, who greeted Sergeant Hanso with a respectful nod or a half-raised hand.

When Seth had first entered the office, Captain Miller shook his hand and complimented him on surviving out in the snowy wastelands. Miller was polite but curt, and it was obvious from the start that he was appraising Seth. His eyes lacked warmth.

Now Seth sat facing him across the desk. The sergeant stood to attention behind and slightly to the left of Miller.

The Captain's hair was combed to one side and he sported an old-fashioned thick moustache, neatly trimmed, with flecks of grey in the black.

His office was sparsely furnished, with only the desk and the two chairs that Miller and Seth sat upon. A framed watercolour of an English wheat field hung on the wall behind the desk. A filing cupboard and a kettle on the side.

Two mugs and a jar of coffee. A standing lamp in the corner. The only items on the desk were a pot of pens, a closed notebook, and a snow globe paperweight. The air smelled of old sweat, but he wondered if that was his own stench.

Seth's hands fidgeted in his lap. He swallowed, glanced at Sergeant Hanso then returned his gaze to Miller, trying not to appear nervous. Trauma and terror had made a nest in his heart.

"What happened to you, Seth?" Miller asked, opening the notebook.

"What do you want to know?" Seth asked, unsure where to begin.

"All of it."

There were elements which brought him shame, but Seth withheld nothing, and when he was done, he sat in the chair with his eyes downcast. There was something cleansing in confession. He waited for Miller to finish scratching his notes.

"Quite a few people have died in order for you to live, wouldn't you say?"

The bluntness of Miller's statement caught Seth off guard, and at first he could only nod and avert his eyes. His mouth and throat were dry and his stomach ached from hunger.

"It's true," said Seth, barely raising his voice above a murmur, ashamed to admit it to stronger men who probably thought him a lucky coward. "I don't know what else to say."

Miller placed his hands together on the desk. One finger

ran over the wedding ring on his other hand. He leaned forward. "A lot of my soldiers gave their lives to save people like you. Sometimes the strong have to die for the weak to live. But in the meantime the weak must grow stronger to take their place. That's how I see it, anyway."

Weak, Seth thought, and looked at the floor. "How far has the snow spread? How bad is the situation?"

"As far as we know, it's everywhere."

"Everywhere?" Seth's guts tightened. He had hoped it was confined to Great Britain. "You mean...?"

"The snow, the monsters, the cold. It's worldwide. I'd heard that the Americans were putting up a fight, especially in the Southern states, but it was a losing battle. Mainland Europe went dark on the first day. The rumours about the Chinese detonating nukes in their own cities couldn't be confirmed."

"Christ," said Seth. One hand went to his mouth. A dull pain pulsed inside his head. He ground his teeth, picturing the Earth afloat in space, covered in ice and snow. A white sphere dying a slow death.

It was a few moments before Seth could speak again. "Does anyone know what caused it?"

"There are a few theories, but nothing can be confirmed. Most who tried to investigate were killed by the beasts. Listen, the cause is not my concern right now; my job is to protect the souls in this bunker. I need to know that you'll follow the rules and not be a problem for us. I've asked the same of every civilian here, and they've all complied. This is a military installation. We've managed to give ourselves a chance, but we need to keep pulling together. Are you with me, Seth? Are you with us?"

"I won't be a problem."

"That's good to hear. You will be expected to help out, of course. To pull your weight."

"With what?" Seth asked. "What are you doing?"

Miller gave a polite smile as cold as his eyes. "We'll let you know when we need you, don't worry."

"Okay."

"I think we're done now."

Seth rose from the chair.

"I hope you settle in quickly, Seth. We have to make the best of a bad situation. We like team players here, don't we, Sergeant?"

"Yes, sir," said Hanso, still looking straight ahead.

CHAPTER THIRTY-FIVE

Andy and Ruby took Seth to the communal showers and waited outside while he washed. The place was deserted, but he still chose to use one of the private stalls. It was heaven, a relief beyond understanding; the warm water washed away the accumulated sweat, grease and grime of the past few days. He used too much soap, and it stung his eyes, but he didn't care. It was so wonderful he cried for a short while, the sound of the shower spray hiding his sobs.

And for a while he put aside his shame and embraced the warmth.

After that, it was time for dinner, and he was shown to the canteen where the population of the bunker gathered for the last meal of the day. Delia and Jack were there. Delia hugged Seth and said she was relieved to see him. Jack gurgled in his carry-cot and looked up at Seth with little interest. But when Seth offered his finger for Jack to wrap his hand around, the infant did so without hesitation and even gave a small smile.

"This place is a sanctuary," said Delia. "I never want to leave."

They lined up for food with the others. Today's dinner was spaghetti bolognese and a slice of unbuttered bread. Water was available from plastic jugs on the tables.

The canteen was larger even than Medical. The civilians were seated at two long tables stretching down the room, while six soldiers sat at a smaller table near the door. In the far corner, Captain Miller, Sergeant Hanso and Doctor

Felton ate at a table too big for just three people. They were deep in conversation, but it was mainly Miller doing the talking. The other soldiers - the privates and an NCO - scoffed down their meals in silence. They looked worn out and pale, dark patches under their eyes. Seth wondered what they had seen since the snow began to fall. They were fighting a war with no chance of winning.

It was all about hiding and surviving, now.

Seth forked the spaghetti into his mouth and chased it with a sip of water. The food was pretty good for a dingy canteen at the end of the world. He looked around as he chewed, observing the other survivors. He recognised a few from Quinn's group, and he wished the brothers had been alive to see the people they'd saved.

They ate quietly, with some muttered conversation. Ruby kissed her silver cross and put it back in her pocket. Andy gave his slice of bread to her, and she placed her hand upon his on the table. Seth noticed a young family, the parents gently encouraging their daughters to eat without spilling the food down the front of their clothes.

There were hardly any old people. Not a man or woman over sixty. And he counted less than a dozen children, including Jack. So few.

Seth swallowed, put down his fork and looked at his plate.

"You all right?" Andy asked him from across the table.

Seth raised his face, tried to give a reassuring smile, but he failed. The nod he offered instead was barely a movement of his head. "I'll be fine."

The concern in Andy's face only faded slightly. "I know it

takes some getting used to, mate. It feels weird to be safe, doesn't it? Especially when you think about all the bad shit that's happened out there."

Delia spooned puree to Jack, resting the boy in the crook of her elbow upon her lap, pretending to ignore their conversation. Jack looked up at her with large eyes, his cheeks rosy red.

"I know," said Seth. "I know." He had so much to say that he might never stop. Instead, he picked up his fork and kept eating.

*

Seth was assigned a bed in Dormitory Two, adjacent to Dormitory One where Andy, Ruby, Delia and Jack slept. He reckoned that Captain Miller was testing him, separating him from the others. Both dormitories, each with enough beds for approximately fifty people, were barely half-full. The other dormitories were empty and unused.

He was given a new toothbrush in a plastic wrapper, and a small bag of toiletries. Military issue. Simple stuff. The basics. Then he lay on his bed, reading a week-old newspaper he'd found nearby. It was one of the tabloids he didn't like, but he found himself full of bittersweet sadness for the messy world before the snow and the cold. Back when his parents and friends had been alive. The everyday news. Politics and social justice. Crime and punishment. The football results from the previous weekend. Such a deep pang of nostalgia and melancholy swept over him that he had to put the newspaper away. So much had changed in such a short space of time.

In some effort to keep a day-night cycle below ground, the lights were turned off at ten o'clock. And with only his head exposed above the blankets, he stared up at the dark of the ceiling, listening to the sniffles and small sounds of others around him. Some were already asleep. A whispered voice said a prayer. On the other side of the room, a woman sobbed.

Seth closed his eyes and wished for sleep, wrapped below the world of cold and monsters.

*

He dreamed of the dead people, those he once knew, and their faces were full of sorrow within the falling snow. They felt wronged; their lives had been snatched away and yet somehow he'd survived.

He begged for forgiveness, but they turned away and faded into the white fog. He was still beseeching them when a monstrous entity emerged from the fog and loomed over him. It was as big as a mountain, coiled and serpentine like something from the Book of Revelations. Its cavernous maw dripped yellowish saliva, teeth jagged and as big as trees. Its skin was sheer black. Smaller insectoid creatures living upon it, like some alien species of parasite.

The God of the Wastelands.

Seth cowered, cried out.

Then he woke up.

CHAPTER THIRTY-SIX

The days bled together without the rise and fall of the sun. Days spent playing board games with Andy, Ruby and Delia, and meandering around the parts of the bunker they were allowed to visit. Many of the other civilians seemed listless, pale and solemn, like ghosts in some kind of in-between place. A population of traumatised survivors. Some sought solace in religion, while others adapted to military rule with barely-hidden contempt. There were complaints about rationing and the duty rosters for housekeeping.

"So, you and Andy have grown close," Seth said to Ruby as they swept the floor of some nameless corridor on what might have been a morning. Andy was off helping in the kitchens.

Ruby stopped sweeping, leaned on her brush and swiped a strand of hair behind one ear. A small smile creased the corners of her mouth. "Yeah, very much so. He's a good man. I might've given up if it weren't for him."

"Is it official, then?"

"Sort of."

"I'm really pleased for you both. Take care of each other. Make the best of things."

"The best of things," Ruby repeated, but in a whisper.

*

Seth settled into a routine. Meals were eaten. The daily

shower stopped being a novelty. He started to become accustomed to the safety of the bunker, but his nerves were still frayed and he was easily startled by loud noises and raised voices.

When he slept, he suffered bad dreams and nightmares born of survivor's guilt. And he woke feeling lonely. It stayed with him throughout the days and only worsened at night.

*

Each day, he visited the chapel. It was a small, plain room. Rows of wooden chairs and prayer cushions faced a lectern, beyond which was a simple altar. Above the altar, a three-foot high cross hung from the wall. Seth sat on a chair, his hands worrying at each other. He bowed his head because it always felt like the correct thing to do.

He was usually alone in the chapel when he visited, and if someone else did enter the room and sat down, he would always leave. His seclusion in the chapel gave him a small measure of peace amidst the desperation and loneliness. A place to contemplate and remember.

He missed the old world: Facebook, Burger King, *Game of Thrones*. The possibility that the bunker was the last bastion of humanity gnawed at him with blunt teeth. It might be the last outpost. He thought about it, shaking his head, seriously considering the notion of extinction.

The weight of all that death upon his shoulders, the debt he owed; it was a burden on his mind, a cancerous knot within him.

There had to be others out there, hiding and waiting. They couldn't be the last people. This was not the swansong of the human race. But he failed to convince himself and just slumped in the chair with his dismal thoughts.

The door opened at the back of the room, and Seth glanced back to see who had entered.

Sergeant Hanso walked down the aisle and sat on a chair in the row opposite. Hanso looked at him then towards the front, his hands held together, but not in prayer. He sighed, cracked his knuckles.

"Strange, isn't it?" the sergeant said.

"What is?"

"People come here to worship, even after everything that's happened. People still looking for help from God, when they've already lost everything. I don't see any sense in it."

"It gives them comfort," said Seth, gazing at the floor between his feet. "Comfort is a rare thing. Let them do what they want with the time they have left."

"God doesn't give a fuck about us. I don't think He's evil, just beyond caring. Maybe we just pissed him off too much over the years and he finally got sick of us."

"Do you think God is responsible for the snow and the monsters?"

"This is just...life, I think."

Seth swallowed to clear the thickness in his throat. His mouth tasted dirty. He looked towards the cross upon the wall. He thought it might have given him some comfort, but there was nothing. Nothing to help or give him guidance. "It seems hopeless, doesn't it?"

Hanso leaned forward in his seat and eyed Seth. "We

received a radio transmission last night."

Seth stared at the sergeant. He blinked. His stomach fluttered. "What? A transmission? From where?"

"Somewhere east of here, a fair distance away. Someone reaching out to us. It was weak, but it was a signal."

"Did you talk to them?"

"It was a woman's voice. The transmission cut out soon after we spoke to her. But not before she told us her coordinates. She said they're some kind of gated community. A place called Moresby."

"I can't believe it."

"We're not alone," said Hanso.

"And you came here just to tell me this...?"

Hanso shook his head. His eyes were grave. "I came here to ask you to be part of the team we're sending."

"Me?"

"Yes."

"Why?"

"Captain Miller doesn't want to risk too many soldiers on the mission - there aren't many of us left, and most are needed to defend the bunker if it's attacked."

"You mean I'm just more expendable than your squaddie mates?"

"Miller thinks you'll be useful out there, as you've spent a lot of time in the wastelands. He told me to say this is your chance to repay the people who died for you. It's not wise to disagree with Captain Miller when it comes to notions of honour and such. He believes you have a moral duty. From his point of view, this is for your own good."

Seth rubbed his eyes with his knuckles, his blood quickening with low anxiety. Yet the thought of staying within the confines of the bunker filled him with a quiet dread. Like it was some kind of purgatory within the earth. A grave for them all.

"Who's going on the mission?" he asked.

"Me, Private Dahl and Private Beckwith. We'll be well armed and equipped. We'll protect you out there."

Seth grunted. "Guns won't do any good against the big ones."

"In that case, we'll just have to stay out of their way."

"Easier said than done. You haven't seen some of the shit I've seen."

"I've seen plenty of bad shit," the sergeant said. "I saw a huge worm swallow a broken-down bus that was being used as a shelter by several families. I was supposed to get them out of there, get them to safety, but I was too late. I had to watch as that fucking worm opened its mouth and..." He broke off and coughed harshly to mask his broken composure.

"I'm sorry," Seth said. "I didn't mean to..."

The edges of Hanso's mouth twitched. His throat worked. "No matter. It's done."

A few moments passed before Seth spoke again. "How long will it take to walk to Moresby?"

"Depending on the conditions, two days or so. It'll be a struggle, Seth. I won't lie to you about it."

Seth shivered and tried to ignore the niggling feeling in his chest. His hands worried at each other, and he winced at the soreness of his knuckles.

Hanso stood, flattening the creases in the front of his fatigues with his palms. "We're leaving in a few days, so you've got a bit of time to prepare yourself. I'll give you some weapons training."

"Okay, I'm in."

"I'll be in touch. Thank you, Seth." Hanso turned away to leave.

"Did I really have a choice?" asked Seth.

The sergeant didn't look back as he walked away. "Not really, but it's polite to ask, isn't it?"

CHAPTER THIRTY-SEVEN

The next day Hanso took Seth through some basic weapons training with a Glock 17. When he first held the pistol in both hands it felt lighter than expected.

They spent a couple of hours at the small shooting range near the soldiers' barracks, Hanso watching while Seth fired at targets. His aim was poor at first, but with practice and a bit of shrewd advice he started to become halfway competent. And by the end of those two hours Seth's arms were aching.

"What do you think?" Seth asked.

"Not bad," said Hanso. "At least those big monsters are hard to miss."

*

The days before leaving passed slowly, with many games of Monopoly played between Seth, Ruby and Andy. They tried to talk him out of going on the mission. Andy even pleaded at one point, but Seth said he'd already promised Hanso, and the sergeant wasn't the kind of man you broke a promise to.

On the night before the day of the mission, Seth lay in bed, away from the others in the dormitory, swamped in darkness, his heart crashing within the wet chamber of his chest. He thought of monsters and death, and the world fading away to be lost in ice and snow. And when he slept eventually, he dreamed of the countless bones of extinct species, bleached white and cold. And atop the pile, a human skull, hollow and grinning.

*

In the morning he was woken by Hanso at his bedside. It was still dark in the dormitory. The only light was from the sergeant's torch, shining towards the floor.

Seth winced, dry-mouthed, and looked up at Hanso. "Is it time?"

"Get dressed and have something to eat. We leave in one hour."

*

It saddened Seth to have no chance to say goodbye to Andy, Ruby, Delia, and baby Jack. He met Hanso and a couple more soldiers near the barracks, where the sergeant gave him a rucksack of equipment and supplies: flares, rope, batteries, bottled water, protein bars. No pistol, but Hanso handed him a long-handled axe with an immaculately sharp edge. It was some consolation.

They all wore heavy winter clothes, boots, and snow goggles. Dark colours. Woollen hats and gloves. Enough layers to keep out the cold.

Hanso pulled on his balaclava and adjusted it for comfort. The sergeant showed no sign of nerves; but when Seth looked at Privates Dahl and Beckwith, their anxiety was clear as they performed their last-minute equipment checks. Dahl was tall and wiry, with red hair and a scar on the left side of his chin, whilst Beckwith was of average height and wide-shouldered, his eyes bloodshot from nerves or lack of sleep. Hanso hefted his own rifle and nodded at the men. They returned the gesture to signal they were ready. Then the sergeant turned to Seth, who was gripping the axe tightly, staring at the steel ladder they'd have to climb.

"You OK, Seth?"

Seth meant to nod, but the muscles in his neck seemed too stiff. He exhaled and gave Hanso a weak half-smile that the sergeant took as an affirmative.

"Let's go, lads," Hanso said. "Sooner we get to Moresby and see what's going on, the sooner we can get back here in the warm."

"Yes, Sarge," Dahl replied.

"On it, Sarge," Beckwith said, and started up the ladder. Dahl followed.

Hanso looked back at Seth. "You're up. Stay close to my lads when you reach ground level. I'll be right behind you."

Seth swallowed, grimacing at the sourness inside his chest and stomach. "Okay. Okay."

"You ready?"

"Yeah."

"Let's go, then."

CHAPTER THIRTY-EIGHT

The silence hit Seth like something physical. He looked around but couldn't see further than forty yards because everything was lost to falling snow and white fog. It was the wasteland in all its terrible glory. Cold and death in the void.

The air was sharp in his nose and mouth. His breath was like smoke, drifting away from him. "Fuck!" It was about all he could say. Icy air cut through his lungs. A gust of wind swept past him.

The soldiers stood nearby, scanning around, their rifles ready. Seth flexed the fingers of one hand on the axe handle. He ran his tongue over his cold teeth. The straps of the rucksack strained on his shoulders.

Sergeant Hanso looked at his men then Seth. "Let's get going, lads. We can't waste daylight."

"I wish we had a snowcat," said Dahl, with a dismal tone.

"Yeah," Beckwith said, sniffling. "Save the effort of walking and there'd be less chance of being eaten."

Hanso shook his head and regarded Seth. "Moaning little bastards, aren't they?"

Seth gave something like a shrug, but said nothing. He shivered, trying to ignore the shrill voice of the wind inside his head.

*

They walked for hours, slogging through the snow on the road, nothing but silence beyond them. Beckwith and Dahl alternated between taking point and bringing up the rear, keeping watch with their rifles half-raised. Neither of them spoke. Seth noticed that Beckwith's rifle was equipped with an under-slung grenade launcher, and he hoped it would do some good against the monsters they would surely encounter. But it didn't make him feel any safer.

Hanso walked beside Seth, checking his map and compass, muttering to himself.

Seth gripped his axe in one hand, eyes flitting about, mouth twitching. The snow crackling under their boots seemed shockingly loud to Seth. It reached past their ankles and, in places where the surface of the road dipped, halfway up their shins.

Seth struggled to keep pace with the soldiers. Dahl urged him onwards from behind.

"You OK, Seth?" Hanso asked him, looking up from the map for a short moment.

Adjusting his goggles against the falling snow, Seth replied, "Yeah, just fine." He kept his voice quiet, as if speaking any louder might summon the monsters. He felt clumsy, awkward and vulnerable, and it was an effort to slow his breathing.

Hanso put away the map and the compass then unslung his rifle, keeping the barrel pointed towards the ground. "I never liked snow that much," he muttered. "Even when I was a kid. Never saw the appeal of it.""I thought all kids liked snow?" said Seth

"I must have been the exception."

"Fair enough." Seth considered asking if Hanso had children, but thought it best not to; the sergeant might be suppressing his own grief and pain. Most people were, he reckoned.

No one spoke for a long while, following the road as it curved eastward. They trudged in slow steps, watchful for threats. The silence was oppressive, full of portent and danger, and not to be trusted.

"I haven't heard any monsters," Beckwith muttered. "I thought they would have come at us by now. Maybe they've fucked off back to wherever they came from."

"I doubt it," said Hanso. "Eyes open, lads."

Beckwith held up one hand and the group stopped. Hanso tensed, raised his rifle. Seth tried to look beyond Beckwith, but he could only see the muddled shapes of cars upon the road.

"What is it?" Hanso asked, and stepped forward.

"Something ahead," said Beckwith.

"Monsters?"

"Something in one of the cars. The one where some of the snow has fallen from its windows. You see it?"

"I see it," Hanso said.

Seth walked with the soldiers as they moved forward, not really wanting to look any closer. But there was no choice, and they stopped next to the car.

"Maybe something shook the snow loose," said Dahl. "Maybe something heavy passed nearby."

The men peered through the nearest window.

A family had taken shelter inside the car, huddling together against the cold on the back seat. A mum and dad, with two children - twin girls no older than ten - wrapped up in their thin coats. Their faces were bone-white. Their eyes were closed, as though they'd simply fallen asleep. The girls wore pink coats with flower patterns, and their blonde hair, glistening with frost, hung rigidly from beneath woollen hats.

Seth tried to imagine their last thoughts as they slipped away into the darkness. His mouth trembled and he stepped back, swallowing the hard clot in his throat. The world went away for a moment.

Beckwith edged his face closer to the window. "Poor bastards. They never had a chance. Still, better this than being eaten alive."

Dahl turned away, shaking his head.

"At least they were together at the end," Hanso said heavily.

CHAPTER THIRTY-NINE

They walked another ten miles before the daylight faded and sent them looking for shelter. Kicking through thick snow, Private Dahl led them towards a house away from the road.

Seth couldn't shake the image of the dead family from his mind, no matter how hard he tried. He kept seeing the girls' faces whenever he closed his eyes.

Dahl and Beckwith unfolded small metal spades from their packs and cleared the snow from the front door. There were no signs of movement within the house, but that didn't mean it was empty. Beckwith opened the front door and went in, his rifle pointed ahead. Dahl followed while Hanso and Seth waited outside on the snow-covered lawn. The tops of dead flowers, pale with frost, poked above the snow. Frozen clothes and thin fingers of ice hung from a washing line.

Seth looked at the upstairs windows. The curtains were drawn. Part of the drainpipe on the front of the house had come loose from its fittings, and now leaned to one side.

Hanso cast about, watching the perimeter. His face set in a frown.

"All clear," Dahl said from inside.

Hanso nodded at Seth and they entered the house. It was a relief when the sergeant closed the door behind them.

*

They stood around the corpse of a man who'd slit his own wrists at his desk in the study. Shelves of old volumes crowded the walls. Model aeroplanes were mounted upon stands. Framed certificates. Hanso snatched the bottle of whiskey from the desk, unscrewed the cap, took a swig. Then, when he noticed Dahl and Beckwith looking at him expectantly, passed the bottle to them. When Beckwith offered Seth the bottle, he drank deeply until the creeping cold was burned from his chest and stomach.

"Secure the house," Hanso said. "This is home for the night."

Beckwith gestured at the dead man. "What about him?"

"Leave him. He's not hurting anyone."

*

Night fell quickly and the wind rose to wailing beyond the walls. They set up camp in the living room at the back of the house, swaddled in their gear and blankets. The soldiers kept their rifles within reach. The battery-powered lantern in the middle of the floor gave a low light, just enough to manifest their shadows.

For dinner they ate MREs - 'Meals Ready to Eat' according to Hanso - followed by protein bars and water from their canteens. The sergeant passed around the whiskey once more. Seth lay his head against the wall and felt the anxiety of the day's journey leak out of him.

He closed his eyes. The family in the car rose from his memories to ask why he hadn't saved them.

*

"I thought Afghanistan was bad," said Beckwith as he picked at his fingernails. "I'd give anything to go back in time, when most of the lads were still alive."

"Amen to that," said Dahl. He ate sparingly from a packet of wine gums while thumbing through a book about the history of Great Britain. "This cold makes Camp Bastion seem like paradise."

Hanso nodded, sipping from his canteen. "We lost some good blokes out there. And back here."

"Are you all from the same unit?" Seth asked.

"Yeah," Hanso replied. "I've known Dahl and Beckwith for a few years. Same with the other lads back at the bunker. We're all that remains of our battalion, most probably." He shook his head dismally, his face wan in the lantern light, then put down the canteen.

The wind screamed outside, harmonising briefly with the creaking of walls and old pipes within the system of the house. It unnerved the men. Seth shivered and shifted in the blankets wrapped around him, trying to ignore the aching of his legs and feet. His bones and joints scraped at the slightest movement, and a shallow pain pressed behind his eyes.

"You look fucked, Seth," said Beckwith.

Seth looked up at the man, who was directly across the room from him. Beckwith's face was pale, his eyes deep set within his skull.

"A bit tired, that's all," said Seth, trying to appear indifferent but failing.

"Reckon you can keep going tomorrow?" There was some amusement in Beckwith's voice. He didn't even bother to disguise it.

"Leave him alone, Beckwith," Dahl said.

Beckwith made a show of mock surprise. "I'm just making conversation."

Dahl shook his head and returned to his book. "Dickhead."

"I'm sure I'll be fine, Beckwith," Seth said. "Thanks for your concern."

Beckwith gave a slight smile, not entirely without humour. "Good to hear. I'm only messing about with you, mate. Don't take it seriously like Dahl does; he's always been sensitive."

Dahl tutted but didn't look up.

Beckwith regarded Hanso. "What's the plan tomorrow, Sarge?"

Hanso exhaled. "We'll set out at first light and keep walking until we find Moresby."

"And then what?" Seth asked.

"We'll see what's waiting for us."

"You think Moresby is legit?" asked Beckwith.

Hanso didn't answer immediately. "I hope so."

"It'll be full of cannibals," Dahl said.

The others looked at him, but he didn't raise his face from the book. Beckwith laughed bitterly. The sergeant merely sighed.

"Time to get some kip," said Hanso. "Dahl, Beckwith and I will take it in turns to be on stag. Four hours each. Dahl, you go first. I'll take the last watch. Anything comes near the house, you know what to do."

"Yes, Sarge," Dahl and Beckwith said together.

Hanso turned to Seth. "Get some shut-eye. Big day tomorrow."

Seth did as he was told, and settled down in his sleeping bag and blankets.

The lantern was turned off and all fell to darkness.

CHAPTER FORTY

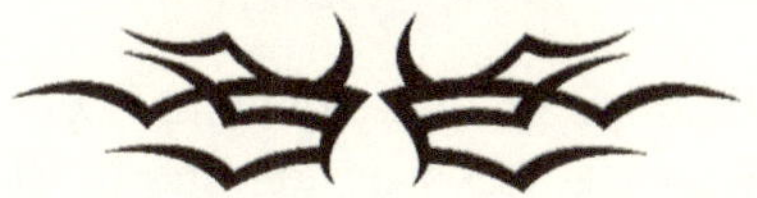

Seth dreamed of his old life: the dead end jobs he'd worked and the old girlfriends he'd dumped; nights out with his mates at pubs and clubs in Yeovil; drunken memories viewed through a haze; the disappointment and love of his parents. Then he dreamed about monsters surrounding the house in the night, and woke in the dark, gasping and clawing at his throat because he thought slick tendrils were strangling him.

He came to his senses with tears in his eyes, shivering in his sleeping bag. He lay there and listened to the low snoring of the soldiers for a while.

Eventually he closed his eyes again and thought about the dead he'd left behind.

*

In the morning, they gathered their things and set out from the house, the snow falling heavy about them through the thick white fog. Utter silence beyond them.

Beckwith took point, while Seth and Hanso followed no more than ten yards behind. Dahl watched the rear. They returned to the road, Hanso making sure they didn't spread too thin as they moved.

Passing through another cluster of abandoned vehicles on the road, Seth noticed an articulated lorry, the trailer of which was open at the back. The doors hung wide, wavering slightly in the wind. He slowed when he heard a faint sound from within the deep shadows.

Behind him, Dahl whispered, "I hear it, too. Is that crying?"

They both stopped, and moments later so did Hanso and Beckwith. They gathered beside one of the snow-shrouded cars, watching the trailer. The crying became louder. It was unmistakeable.

"What the fuck?" said Beckwith.

"It can't be a child, can it?" Dahl muttered. "It couldn't have survived out here."

"I don't know," said Seth.

Hanso switched on the small torch attached to the underside of his rifle's barrel. "Wait here, lads. Cover me." He moved into position and trained his rifle upon the back of the trailer. Dahl moved a few paces to his left and did the same, clearing a line of fire. Seth could only stand and watch Hanso approach the trailer. His hands tightened on his axe. His mouth tensed.

The wind died down until it was nothing but a cold breath.

Hanso stood before the open back of the trailer and raised his rifle. The torchlight speared the darkness within and revealed the insides, encrusted with dried blood and bones. And amidst it all lurked a pale arachnid thing of bulbous flesh and thin crooked limbs. It was as big as a horse. Multiple black eyes squirmed together, glistening and wet, pierced with red pupils. A slavering mouth quivered, mimicking a child's cry.

The skin of the creature's body bristled with thick, white hair.

"Holy fuck," Beckwith said.

The arachnid scuttled towards the open back of the trailer, moving straight for Hanso.

"Run," Seth whispered to the sergeant.

Hanso stepped back and fired his rifle.

The pale arachnid screeched.

Hanso reeled away as it darted towards him. And it would have speared him with one of its sharply-tipped front limbs if Dahl and Beckwith hadn't opened fire with their rifles, expending their magazines in mere moments. The sheer rate of fire sent it fleeing through the clotted ranks of abandoned cars, its skittering limbs working nightmarishly fast and ragged.

Dahl and Beckwith reloaded. Hanso returned with his rifle aimed at the last place the arachnid had been seen.

"Well, that was fucked up," said Beckwith.

Dahl shrugged. "I never liked spiders. You OK, Sarge?"

"Almost shat myself," Hanso said.

There was stifled laughter from Beckwith, but Hanso silenced him with a stern look.

The soldiers formed a defensible perimeter between two abandoned cars, sweeping the immediate area with their rifles. Seth stayed in the centre, holding his axe with both hands, feeling immensely foolish for leaving the bunker.

The sound of a crying child drifted out once more from the white fog and falling snow.

"Eyes open," Hanso told them.

"Yes, Sarge," said Beckwith and Dahl.

Seth looked towards the trailer. There was black blood in the snow outside the opened back. "You hurt it."

"I should fucking hope so!" said Beckwith. "We put enough rounds into the fucking thing."

"Be quiet," said Hanso, as the thing cried out again. But there was no sign of it. No movement. No glimpse of those black eyes staring back at them. Then the sound stopped. Seth thought he glimpsed a flash of motion off to his right and turned towards it, but there was nothing.

"Where the fuck is it?" Beckwith whispered, scanning the white fog. Despite the tensing of his body, he gripped his rifle lightly, almost casually. A professional soldier, just like Hanso and Dahl.

The arachnid leapt towards them from out of the veils of fog and falling snow. The soldiers fired their rifles and scattered. Seth tried to move with them, but in the confusion of the creature's attack he fell against one of the cars and sagged to his knees, winded and gasping. He heard Beckwith cry out from somewhere nearby, followed by more rifle fire that rang in his ears. He glanced about, panicked, but he couldn't see the soldiers anywhere. The axe trembled in his hands as he sought better cover.

More rifle fire around him. It sounded distant, and suddenly he was terrified that he'd been left behind, alone with the nightmare creature.

A stray bullet hit the bonnet of the car next to him, only a few feet from his head. "Shit!" he cried, crouching out of sight.

The spider-thing lunged at him from his left, appearing from behind a black van. He dove to the side. The tip of one of its sharp limbs impacted where he'd just been crouching, kicking up granules of snow. He landed on his backside, shouting for help. The creature's mouth snapped at him, and he swung his axe, embedding the blade in soft, pulpy flesh. He lost his grip as the arachnid screeched and reared, trying to shake the axe free. Black blood dribbled from the wound in its face. Its crooked legs twitched and stamped.

Seth could only sit on his arse and stare at the monstrous thing until a hand grasped his shoulder and began pulling him away through the snow. He glanced back at Dahl, who merely nodded at him. Hanso and Beckwith appeared with their rifles aimed at the wailing monster.

The roar of gunfire was deafening. Dahl let go of Seth, and he climbed awkwardly to his feet to watch. The beast sagged, bleeding and broken, legs twisted and crumpled.

Finally, it stilled.

The men stood staring at the fallen monster until Hanso got them moving again. The din would attract attention, and other things would soon arrive to scavenge the monster's corpse.

CHAPTER FORTY-ONE

The snow was falling quicker, heavy and hindering. The fog had closed in. Seth trampled on the spot to keep warm, arms wrapped around his chest. Exhaustion made a heavy weight upon his mind and body. The blood felt slow inside his veins and arteries.

Hanso took point and led them down a straight road until they reached some tall iron gates set in a high wall that stretched away to either side. The gates were secured by a wrapped chain and padlock. The snow had been recently cleared from the entrance by the looks of it.

They exchanged uncertain glances at this apparent welcome. Beckwith and Dahl kept their rifles ready, watching their flanks, while Hanso and Seth went up to the gates and peered between the black railings. The shapes of houses and parked cars were dark and muddled in the encroaching fog. Gardens were buried in snow. The gangly forms of tall trees at the sides of the avenue led away from them into whiteness.

Hanso took off his goggles and left them hanging around his neck. He squinted past the gates.

"What do you think?" Seth asked him.

"Looks deserted."

"But someone obviously cleared the snow from the gate."

"I know. Shouldn't there be a bell to ring or something?"

"What we doing, Sarge? What we gonna do?" Beckwith said from behind them. Dahl sighed at Beckwith's impatience.

Hanso opened his mouth to answer, when a lone figure emerged from the fog. A woman. She was tall, thin, and clad in a long coat. Her face, initially obscured within the furred hood, was only revealed when she came closer to the gates. It was gaunt, pallid. She halted, held her hands together at her waist, and smiled at the men. It was a welcoming smile, almost matronly, but the edges of it trembled and looked damp. There was a sort of hopefulness in her eyes. She appeared to be in her forties or early fifties. She reminded Seth of his Aunt Jane, and then he realised he was smiling back at her.

"I'm so glad you made it," she said. "You must have heard me over the airwaves. You answered my call. Thank you so much."

Hanso looked at Seth then back to the woman. "Who are you? What is this place?"

Her smile never faded as she took a key from her coat pocket. "My name is Eve. Welcome to Moresby. I hope you'll feel at home here."

CHAPTER FORTY-TWO

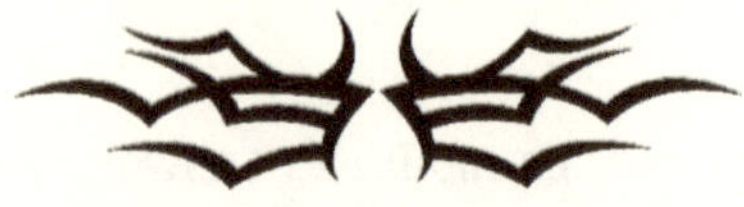

Eve gave them entrance through the gates and led them along the main road into the gated community. Hanso and Seth walked either side of her. Dahl and Beckwith followed several paces behind. They trudged through the snow, past houses and cars, all abandoned and shrouded in powdery white. Darkened windows full of shadows looked out at them.

"It's just me and a few others here," Eve said.

"How many others?" asked Seth.

"Six others, aside from myself. There around here somewhere."

Seth and the soldiers glanced around. "That's all there are?"

The sense of disappointment was obvious amongst the men. Beckwith looked glum. Dahl's face was impassive.

"We thought there was a community here," said Hanso, casting his eyes about at the empty places. "We hoped there'd be more survivors."

"I'm sorry to disappoint you," Eve told them. "There were more of us, but they went away."

"Where did they go?"

She looked towards the sky, but only for a second. "I can't remember. Things are different out here."

"Do you have electricity?"

"We've been transmitting through a battery-powered short wave radio set. We're on the last lot of batteries."

They approached the centre of Moresby. The snow seemed to fall heavier here, where the silent houses lined the street. And it all felt oppressive and hostile to Seth, as if he and the soldiers were encroaching on enemy territory. He shook his head to dispel the notion, tried his best to drag up some hope in his heart, but there was only the cold inside him, spreading, taking him over.

"Where are the other survivors?" Seth whispered to Hanso, who just stared straight ahead and raised his rifle. The sergeant was the first to see the towering creature that appeared out of the white fog ahead of them. Something black and colossal, as big as a mountain and tall enough that its massive form continued up into the clouds.

They halted, all of them, staring up towards it. Seth's breath caught in his throat and he almost dropped the axe.

"Holy shit," was all Hanso said.

From what Seth could see, it was an immense serpent-like beast coiled in inconceivable mounds. It was the biggest thing Seth had seen yet in the cold; maybe the largest creature to ever inhabit the planet. A destroyer of worlds. Seth felt like dust by comparison. He was nothing.

The beast had made a nest by flattening buildings and digging into the ground to immerse part of its unimaginable bulk. Its head wasn't visible, hidden higher up by the fog, or tucked away within its black coils, most of which were covered with ridges, spikes and scales. Its slumbering respiration trembled in the ground. Drifts of snow had settled upon the slopes of its coiled form.

Seth had seen it in his dreams during his last night at

the bunker. He remembered them now. His insides crumpled. His hands shook. He felt the urge to run away, out into the wastes beyond Moresby, and let the snow bury him.

Sergeant Hanso turned to Eve, his face taut with dread and something like awe. "What the fuck is that thing?"

Eve gazed up at the immense creature in pure adulation. Seth answered for her.

"The God of the Wasteland."

CHAPTER FORTY-THREE

Seth's voice was weak in the presence of the God. He winced at the nausea in the back of his mouth. "I saw it in a dream."

The soldiers looked at him in utter confusion.

"He wants you all to worship Him," Eve said.

Hanso spat on the ground.

"That thing?" gaped Beckwith. "Are you fucking mad?"

Eve pawed absently at her mouth as she stared up at the creature. "Worship or die."

Beckwith and Dahl looked to Hanso, hoping he'd take charge, but the sergeant appeared dumbfounded.

"Will you stay with me?" Eve asked the men. "Won't you stay?" She glanced at each of them before her gaze settled on Seth.

"You," she said to him. "You had the dream. You saw the glory of it all. Do you want to turn your back on the God?"

"It's not like that," Seth said, trying to hide the tremor in his voice. "Maybe you should come back with us?"

"You dreamt about that thing?" Hanso asked Seth, who only nodded.

The soldiers looked at him with distrust.

"I belong here," said Eve, her face flushing with anger. Her neck muscles twitched. "And so do you all. Those who've had the dream will be the acolytes of the God of the Wasteland. We will watch Him devour the infidels."

Seth found himself drawn, in some horrid fashion, to Eve's way of thinking. It was an attractive ideology to weak minds and desperate people. He'd craved acceptance and vindication in his old life, and he still did now, even from insane zealots in the howling wastes. Suddenly he remembered his job interview on the last morning of the old world and gritted his teeth against a sense of seething injustice and self-loathing.

He was tempted to join Eve, as if her zealotry was contagious, but he suppressed the urge, shaking his head. He looked at her with pleading in his eyes. "Come with us. Leave the God behind. No one should be out here alone with that creature."

Eve just stared back at him.

"You trying to save her?" Beckwith said, glaring at Eve. His hands tightened around his rifle. "We slogged all this way for this bullshit? We should leave her here."

"Calm down, Beckwith," said Dahl. He was the closest to Eve, watching her carefully.

"Fuck that. Attacked by an overgrown fucking spider and freezing our arses off. Fuck all this. Fuck all that. Fuck this maniac bitch."

"Shut up, Beckwith," Hanso ordered.

Eve began to tremble and judder with what seemed like rage or grief. Tears welled in her eyes. Despite her frail appearance, she was fast - and before they could react she pulled a short-bladed knife from one sleeve of her coat.

Her hand rose towards Dahl, and she lunged at him and

slashed across his throat. Blood splashed down the front of Dahl's coat as Eve stepped away with her hands raised in celebration. Dahl slumped to his knees, gasping and choking, clutching the red ruin of his throat. He fell onto his back to stare up at the sky, shuddering as the life leaked from him. Blood pooled around his cooling body.

All of it had happened in seconds.

Eve screamed, glared at them with wild eyes, ready to attack again.

Beckwith raised his rifle and shot her twice in the head. At such close range, the back of her skull exploded, spitting blood and brain. She toppled over, dropping the knife onto the reddening snow.

No one said a word. The reports echoed in Seth's ears. Beckwith crouched next to Dahl, but the man was already dead; his arms lay loose at his sides. Eyes open. His mutilated throat glistened.

"Mate," Beckwith whispered as he bowed his head. "That fucking bitch. I'm sorry, mate. I'm so sorry. Stupid crazy fucking bitch." He stood and looked back at Seth and Hanso, but their attention was taken by several dozen human figures standing some distance away, at the coiled base of their God. Men, women and children. They cried out as they stared up at the God, then stepped forward as one, and disappeared into its immense bulk, as though they'd been absorbed. Their cries fell to dreaded silence.

"We shouldn't have come here," said Beckwith.

The ground began to rumble, and the respirations of the God-thing paused. The snow thickened in the air.

A deep, reverberating wail fuelled by cavernous lungs

broke the silence and had the men covering their ears. They staggered away from the God as its immense cry rose into the air and echoed throughout the abandoned community. Houses shook on their foundations. Windows shattered.

The drifts of snow upon the monster's coils shifted and fell away as it began to emerge from its slumber with elongated tendrils writhing. The sound of grinding rock and earth. Tremors in the ground.

Seth could only stare in horrid fascination, before Hanso and Beckwith grabbed him and pulled him away.

The God rose from its nest.

CHAPTER FORTY-FOUR

Beckwith blew the gates open with one shot from his grenade launcher, and the men fled Moresby, kicking through the snow in a panicked, terrified fugue. Seth glanced back at the terrible place as the black shape of the God seemed to dominate the sky. It was enough to bring him close to madness and tears.

"Oh Christ," he muttered, panting and gritting his teeth. "Oh fucking hell."

"Keep moving," Hanso said, pushing him on. "Stop looking back!"

The wailing of the God scraped at the insides of Seth's skull. The world was all blaring sound and terror. Beckwith was shouting, his words inaudible, his face wild as if rage and hysteria filled his blood. Hanso wheezed and grunted with exertion, urging them onwards.

The ground trembled, shook the men off balance and sent them staggering through the veils of falling snow. They stumbled and flailed, afraid to even slow down, all the while expecting the God to bear down on them and crush their bodies into red pulp.

And they kept going, never stopping, never looking back in case the looming bulk of the serpentine God was the last thing they ever saw.

*

They stopped twenty minutes later and hid in the enclosed garden of a bungalow not far from the road, crouching behind a wooden fence as the bestial cries of the God echoed all around.

"I don't want to die out here," Beckwith whispered, hugging his rifle tight to his chest. Hanso looked at the sky, his eyes full of despair, his mouth open in shock.

*

They walked again, and eventually returned to the house they'd sheltered in on their way to Moresby. As before, they set up camp in the living room as the darkness moved in, wrapped in their blankets, eating their meagre provisions. They said nothing for a long while. Seth was glad of the silence; it felt as if his mind was recovering from merely being in the presence of the God. His body shivered with aches. Lactic acid broiled in his limbs.

They were all distraught and exhausted.

"All this way for nothing," said Hanso. "Just to lose Dahl. For nothing."

"He was my mate," said Beckwith, staring at the floor, chewing his food slowly. His eyes were distant.

Hanso nodded. "He was a good soldier. A good mate. We'll drink for him when we get back to the bunker."

"How many lads have we lost, Sarge?"

"Too many," Hanso said.

"How long do you think *we* have left?"

"Don't talk like that."

"Why not? It's inevitable, isn't it? Surely the only choice we have is *how* we die? There's nothing else left."

Hanso looked away, unable to answer. Seth glanced at

Beckwith, saw the dampness of the soldier's eyes and the frailty of his mouth. Maybe Beckwith was right.

*

In the morning they left the house. They walked in silence, ever watchful, hunching over like miserable vagrants. Each breath scraped itself from Seth's chest and his legs felt heavy. A damp knot pulsed behind his sternum. His stomach ached. It was all he could do just to put one foot in front of the other. Hanso helped him on while Beckwith took point.

The snow fell heavy and fast.

No monsters came for them, but the keening of the God drifted to them from an unseen place far away, a reminder that this world now belonged to beasts of nightmare and fevered visions.

*

It took all day to reach the bunker, and by the time they were allowed entry by Captain Miller, they were miserable and beyond exhaustion. Seth had to be helped down the ladder shaft and half-carried to Medical, where he passed out.

CHAPTER FORTY-FIVE

His dreams were of fear, pain, and immense shapes that burst from drifts to rule the world. He saw mountains of bones stretching toward the horizon underneath a sky of darkness, where a weakened sun bled out the last of its warmth. There was nothing but the cold and the new Gods of the dying Earth.

He woke to faint echoes of screams, gunshots and panicked cries. Doctor Felton stood over him. He sat up, panting. The dampness had cleared from his chest. He was wearing a fresh t-shirt and underwear, but the smell of his stale sweat was pungent. He looked around. Much of the medical equipment in the room was scattered over the floor, along with sheets of paper and shattered jars.

The doctor was scratching at his wrist, face slack and clammy with terror. The walls of Medical shuddered and dust fell from the ceiling. It sounded as if the bunker was caught in an earthquake, but of course it was something else. The realisation was almost enough to almost stop his heart.

Felton wiped at his damp mouth. His hands trembled. "It's broken through the top of the bunker already. I saw it take some people; just snatched them up through the ceiling."

Seth looked at the doctor, grimacing as the room shook again. "It must have followed us back here."

"Why would it do that?"

"We rejected it. It's a God. Maybe it's got a fragile ego. I don't know."

"We can't stay here," Felton said, grabbing several satchels of medical supplies and slinging them over his shoulders. He winced and straightened out the straps. "The civilians are heading to the lower levels. We need to go, Seth. There isn't much time."

Seth climbed out of the bed and dressed in the clothes that'd been piled beside him. He pulled on the thick coat and boots last. "How long has it been, since we returned?"

"Two days. Sergeant Hanso told us what happened at Moresby. A wasted effort. Such a shame. But now we have to go."

"It'll kill us all," said Seth.

"The soldiers are fighting it."

"It won't matter."

*

The corridors were busy with people fleeing towards the lower levels. Some of them were staggering with injuries, while others carried bags of food and water. Shocked, frantic expressions on every face. A man cried with nothing but a photo album in his hands. The corridor juddered. The lights flickered. Distant grinding sounds, the twisting of metal, all became louder until they were drowned out by rapid gunfire from the direction of the upper levels. Seth looked that way then back to Felton, flinching at a detonation from one of the levels above.

"Where are Andy and Ruby?" Seth asked the doctor.

He didn't look at Seth. "I don't know. I haven't seen

them. Come on, we need to leave."

Part of the ceiling above them shattered and collapsed, concrete and rubble raining down. It separated them. Dust billowed, scratching Seth's throat. Felton shouted something but Seth had fallen into a fit of coughing. He only noticed the black tendrils bursting through the hole at the very last moment. They were swift and sleek, grasping blindly for him.

He retreated in slow steps, keeping his breathing low, his eyes trained upon the tendrils, then he pivoted and ran with all the strength he could gather.

The walls shook with violent tremors.

CHAPTER FORTY-SIX

A few minutes later, Seth encountered Hanso and another soldier moving along one of the corridors. They were the first people he'd seen since fleeing from the tendrils. Both soldiers appeared exhausted and harassed, sweating in their thick coats as they reloaded their rifles.

"You're still alive then," Hanso said to Seth, with a curt nod.

"Only just," Seth replied, glancing back the way he'd come.

Hanso gave a grim smile. "The God of the Wasteland has come for us all. Those fucking tendrils are everywhere." He took his pistol from its holster and handed it to Seth. "You're in the army now, lad. You remember your training?"

Seth looked at the gun in his hands then back to Hanso. "The important bits, yeah."

"Good."

"Is this wise, Sarge?" the other soldier said.

"Yes, Marwood." Hanso fixed the private with a hard stare. "We need all the help we can get. Is there an objection?"

Marwood shrugged, glanced at Seth, and then made a show of checking his rifle. "Not at all, Sarge."

"Good. Let's go."

"Where are we going?" Seth said.

"To find Captain Miller."

They moved through the corridors while the walls shook and a great shrieking echoed through the bunker. The gunfire died down for a little while, and then started up again in short bursts. Seth's heart jolted when the lights flickered; the thought of facing those squirming tendrils down here in the dark made his bladder tighten. He struggled to gather saliva in his mouth, and the taste of something sour on his tongue made him queasy.

He noticed more jagged holes and rents in the ceilings, and kept his eyes on them as he passed beneath, fully expecting writhing horrors to fall upon them.

The bunker shuddered within the earth.

*

Moments later they rounded a corner in the corridor and halted before the sight of a beetle-like creature the size of a large pig, feeding on a dead man's entrails. His body was covered in puncture wounds from the beetle's pincer-edged mouth.

The creature hadn't noticed them, and continued to dine on the man's spilled guts. It perched upon the man's chest, its jaws snapping and pulling at coils of viscera.

"Where did that fucking thing come from?" Marwood whispered.

Hanso levelled his rifle at the creature. "Must have come through one of the holes. Means we might have more than those tendrils to worry about."

Marwood wiped his greasy lips. "Fuck's sake."

The beetle jerked its head upwards and hissed.

"Ugly bastard," said Hanso, and fired a three-round burst at the creature.

The beetle flew backwards and landed on its back upon the floor. Its legs twitched and kicked for a moment before Hanso walked over and finished it with one bullet to its gore-soaked head.

They continued towards the distant sound of gunfire.

*

People stumbled past them in the corridors, too terrified and panicked to stop. Parents dragged at crying children. A woman clutched one side of her face as she sobbed and staggered into the shadows of an adjoining corridor. Screams echoed past shaking walls. Seth noticed cracks in the ceilings, and shuddered at the thought of being buried alive down here, trapped and helpless, as the God's tendrils snaked towards him. He would be a small meal.

The sound of gunfire grew louder, and the numbers of fleeing civilians dwindled until it was just Seth, Hanso and Marwood moving along the corridor.

Moments later, they found Captain Miller and four other soldiers - Beckwith, Rourke, Bright, and Leeds - fighting a rearguard action against a swarm of black tendrils spilling forth from the doorway of the communal canteen. Their rifles barked fire, raking the tendrils and delaying their incursion deeper into the bunker. But the bunker was already breached in numerous places, Seth realised. It was futile, no more than an annoyance to the God.

Empty shell casings littered the floor. The smell of gunpowder was thick and acrid. And beneath that, the stink of the oily tendrils was ever-present, like the taint of sewage and rotting things.

Hanso and Marwood joined the others, and at a distance of less than thirty yards opened fire upon the doorway as the black tendrils squirmed and slithered outwards. Seth watched the wretched appendages sway and flap down the corridor, crammed together, all slick and vicious, sharp tips arrowing towards the men.

Miller ordered them to fall back. Leeds and Marwood grabbed Seth and pulled him along, while Rourke, Beckwith, Bright, and Sergeant Hanso provided covering fire. Seth glanced back to see the black tendrils closing upon the men, barely held back by the hail of bullets.

Rourke's rifle ran empty and, as he attempted to reload a whip-thin tendril snapped forward to coil around his right ankle. He was yanked off of his feet, his rifle spilling from his hands, and he screamed as he was dragged into the frothing wave of tendrils, never to be seen again. He was shredded and torn into slopping parts. His blood and intestines coated the tendrils, and their darting movements were galvanised.

Hanso's rifle went empty in his hands as he backed away. He let it swing from its strap to free his hands then grabbed a grenade from his belt. He pulled the pin, glanced back at Seth for a second, and lobbed the grenade into the writhing mass.

Pounding feet on the floor as the men fled. The scraping sounds of the tendrils writhing through the corridor, towards the meat they craved.

The detonation in the enclosed space was thunder and metallic screams.

CHAPTER FORTY-SEVEN

Hanso slammed the door on the smouldering corridor and then piled two wooden chairs against it. He turned back to Seth and the others, his face grim as he reloaded his rifle. They said nothing. Seth's ears were ringing.

Captain Miller stood in the middle of the corridor, sweating and panicked. His icy eyes had turned to water. Marwood and Leeds were staring at the barricade, rifles raised. Distant crashes echoed from somewhere in the bunker.

"What are your orders, Captain?" Hanso asked.

"We fall back and hold those things at bay," muttered Miller. "Protect the civilians." He couldn't hold Hanso's gaze.

"This place is infested," said Seth. "We should evacuate."

Miller snapped at Seth. "If we abandon this place, we'll die out in the wastelands."

"Sir, with respect," Hanso said, "Seth might have a point."

Miller raised his voice. "It's out of the question."

"Why?" Seth asked.

"Because there is nowhere else to go."

Hanso stepped forward, moving away from the barricaded door. There were no sounds from beyond now.

No scraping or scratching in the adjacent corridor. The grenade had apparently done its job.

But it was a minor victory, Seth knew. They all knew.

"We can't beat this thing," Hanso said. "We can hold it off for a while, but it'll get through to us in the end."

"We are not abandoning our post," said Miller. A muscle twitched in his face. "My orders were to hold this bunker, to keep people alive. The line must be drawn!"

"Madness," murmured Seth.

Miller regarded Seth with something like his old, cold fury. "You're a civilian; you have no idea what you're talking about. We will repel this monster and it is not up for fucking discussion!"

Thick cracks appeared directly above Miller, and the stretch of ceiling exploded. Black tendrils fell swiftly and snatched Miller. He only managed to fire a single burst from his rifle before he was pulled through the pitch black rent. His screams were heard for several seconds after he had vanished into the darkness above.

Hanso and Beckwith unloaded their magazines into the cavity hoping to spare his suffering.

The sounds of the bunker's destruction were loud and terrible around them.

*

They moved through deserted corridors. Hanso took charge and led from the front. Seth stayed alongside him, holding the pistol in shaking hands. He kept it pointing downwards, just as Hanso had taught him.

The plan was to evacuate the bunker and escape.

They found a few civilians hiding in darkened rooms; traumatised people who regarded the soldiers with slackly staring eyes and bloodless faces. Clutching bags and belongings, wearing winter clothes. They thanked the soldiers and joined the group, huddling together for protection.

Farther on, the group stopped at the sound of familiar voices in a storeroom. Seth's heart swelled for a moment as he opened the door. Then he saw the blood.

Delia was sitting with her back against the far wall, her hands held over a glistening wound in her stomach. Her face was white, her mouth open, each breath pulled slowly from her chest with damp rattling.

Andy and Ruby crouched nearby. Ruby held Jack in her arms.

Seth went inside, closely followed by the sergeant. Andy stood, gave a small nod and sad shrug of his shoulders. His face was bloodless. Ruby made comforting sounds to Jack.

Far away, rumbles like detonations arose and faded away, but the grinding about them continued, and the walls shuddered. Hanso raised his rifle towards the ceiling when a small burst of grey dust billowed downwards, but no cracks yet appeared in the plaster. Seth held his breath for a drawn out moment, looking upwards.

"Some kind of insect-thing attacked her," Andy said. "I killed it." His mouth stayed open, but he said nothing more. Tears pooled in his eyes. He looked to Delia. Her head dipped to her chest. She muttered something.

Hanso knelt by the woman and peered into her eyes. They were dull and watery. Then he checked her wound, gingerly moving her hand to one side first. She barely resisted. He looked at Seth and Andy, shaking his head.

"Please," Delia whispered, struggling to find the strength to talk. "Look after Jack. Keep him safe. Take care of him."

Hanso placed his hand on her arm, a paltry gesture of comfort.

She glanced at Hanso's rifle, then at him. And Hanso nodded.

"Okay," he said, standing. "Okay."

Seth eyes widened. Ruby stood and went to Andy; he kissed her on the forehead. Everyone looked at the sergeant.

"It's probably best that you all go out in the corridor," he murmured.

They said goodbye to Delia. She kissed Jack's forehead one last time, and gave him a smile. Then they went out to wait with the others. The door closed. No one spoke.

Seconds later a single shot rang out, and that was that.

CHAPTER FORTY-EIGHT

Hanso, Leeds and Seth led the way. Beckwith and Marwood walked at the back of the group, keeping the stragglers moving.

They went on through the twisting maze of corridors, moving in silence.

There were cracks in the walls, in the floors, in the ceilings. A terrible grinding within the ground, mixed with the wailing from the God of the Wastelands as it worked its sinuous way into the structure. Seth pictured the massive creature wrapping itself around the bunker, making a new nest, full of morsels inside for it to consume.

Ruby was trying to calm Jack, who cried in her arms, squirming within his blanket. Andy walked with them. Seth looked over at him and nodded. Andy tried to smile, but his eyes flitted ahead and his mouth trembled.

Distant sounds of scraping rose from behind them.

Farther on, they found a man hanging from a rope on a ceiling light fixture. They stood there a moment, staring at him, none of them saying a word. What could be said?

They walked on.

Hanso brought the group to a stop later, when they came to a corridor carpeted with more than a dozen broken corpses. Large puncture wounds perforated their stomachs and chests. Strips of their clothes had been ripped away and scattered on the floor around them. Doctor Felton lay among the dead.

Hanso pointed his rifle down the corridor and started forward grimly. "Come on. We're not far from the exit."

The others followed, tenderly stepping between or around the corpses. No one spoke. Seth looked down at one of the bodies. It was a young woman, and he noticed that her stomach was trembling. He paused, horrified, and Andy and Ruby walked into the back of him.

"What's wrong?" Andy said."

Memories of the service station burned through him but Seth was paralysed. A small squeaking noise was all he could muster.

Hanso looked back at them, frowning.

Seth couldn't look away from the woman's stomach. It almost seemed like he was willing it to bulge upwards. And then it did, pulsing and tearing swiftly. Something slick, squirming and eel-like emerged from its chamber of flesh, snapping at the air with its sharp mouth. It was the size of a house cat, with pale yellow skin, white eyes, a narrow snout, and three stubby limbs on each side of its elongated body. A low hissing came from between its wicked jaws.

Before anyone could react, the eel-thing leapt from the woman's stomach and sprung towards a man standing beside Andy. The man went down screaming, collapsing to his knees as his hands pawed at the creature. Other people backed away from him, stumbling on the corpses, falling against the walls in an effort to get away. Screams rang out. Jack's cries grew louder.

Within seconds, several of the other corpses began to jerk and shudder, and their stomachs birthed similar monsters.

The soldiers opened fire.

Some of them were blown apart before they could escape their flesh-and-bone nests, but several were too quick and they fell upon the civilians. Chaos followed. Screams and cries. Flailing arms and elbows. Blood sprayed from faces and throats. Seth was pushed face first into the wall by people clamouring to escape. Something like a knee slammed into his lower back and the air was driven from his lungs. He fell to one knee. He turned to see one of the creatures perched upon the struggling form of a woman, who was barely keeping it at bay with her hands. Its mouth was biting at the air inches from her neck. She cried out as her eyes met Seth's.

He raised his pistol, heart stammering, hands shaking, and took aim at the creature.

The loud report was brutal, but the bullet took the eel-thing in the abdomen and sent it flying against the opposite wall. It writhed and shrieked on the floor there, thin tail thrashing. Seth stumbled across the corridor and shot it again, in the face. His hands thrummed from the recoil.

All around him, struggling bodies and shrieking monsters. Bullets pierced the air. Another of the creatures skittered towards him. He shot it four times and when all was done, he stood amid the carnage and looked around.

Ruby was sitting on the floor, away from the bodies, holding tight to Jack, whose cries eventually softened to murmurs. Andy crouched beside them, his arms around Ruby's shoulders. Hanso stood nearby, the barrel of his rifle smoking. Blood spattered his fatigues and thick coat.

The air stank of burnt flesh and gunpowder. A faint taint of urine. The bunker shook in a series of hammering tremors.

The eel-things he could see were dead, but Seth wasn't sure they were all accounted for. Some of them could well have escaped. The group had lost ten people, including Private Marwood. Most of his face was gone, ripped away by savage teeth. Private Leeds crouched beside him and gently plucked the spare magazines from his webbing. Privates Beckwith and Bright looked down at Marwood, their shoulders slumping, faces slack with grief.

"We have to keep going," said Hanso.

They all turned to him. There were some complaints from the civilians, but they knew he was right. The survivors had to go on.

Then the lights went out.

CHAPTER FORTY-NINE

The soldiers activated the torches on their rifles. The few civilians with torches did the same. The corridor was full of the sound of nervous breathing and barely restrained panic, blending with the click and scrape of rifles being reloaded.

People were sobbing in the dark, cowering together or against the walls. They were shadows until the torchlight swept over them, revealing faces full of fear. Beckwith and Leeds began urging them, not unkindly, to get moving again, and they responded in numb reluctance, slowly gathering together again to face down the corridor.

Dazed and vague, Seth looked at the pistol in his hand. He'd killed two of those creatures, but when he tried to remember it all, his mind came up blank. Something to do with trauma and the chemicals in his brain. He shook his head to help clear his thoughts. Ruby stood with Jack still in her arms, holding him tight with something akin to reverence. Like he was a little bundle of hope for all of them.

"We're not far from the exit point," Hanso said to the survivors. "We just have to keep going."

No one protested. It was a silent understanding between them all.

"Let's go," Beckwith said from the back. "Move your arses."

Seth picked up a dropped torch from the floor. He

switched it on, the beam pointing at his blood-splattered boots.

"Come on," Private Bright told the civilians, his voice uneven and strained. "Do as the Sarge says."

As they started down the corridor, a terrible grinding rose from behind them; it grew louder and mixed with the sounds of slick movement. They all looked anxiously back with their torches, peering at the point where the corridor curved into shadow. Someone whimpered. Someone else stifled a gassy, nervous burp.

A cluster of black tentacles emerged from the darkness back there. The limbs of the God, as though the writhing appendages had detached from the shadows to hunt down their prey. They filled the corridor, swaying and thrashing. It was a ghastly, awe-inspiring sight.

"Run!" Hanso said. "Fucking move!"

The civilians ran while Beckwith and Leeds opened fire on the tendrils as they closed in. One of the tendrils snapped forward and wrapped around Leeds' head, lifting him from his feet. He dropped his rifle and beat at the tendril over his face, his screams muffled, his legs kicking at the air.

Beckwith backed away, still putting down fire, but powerless to help Leeds. Moments later Leeds stopped screaming as the tendril tightened around his head and popped his skull like an overripe fruit. Blood and brain matter splashed the ceiling and he was dragged away into the mass of tendrils.

Beckwith fled, firing blindly over his shoulder, lost to panic and terror.

Seth was swept along in the rush of bodies, jabbed and nudged by errant limbs. He kept the pistol clenched in his hand. He heard Beckwith's rifle firing, and then fall silent. He didn't look back.

The trembling of the corridor grew until the group could barely stay on their feet. Thin cracks appeared in parts of the ceiling. The bunker was coming apart.

Seth stumbled against a wall, grazing the back of one hand. He kept going, staggering blindly in the scrum of people. Screams filled his ears. Flailing arms and kicking legs.

The floor split open with a deafening crack. Concrete dust and bullet-sized debris flew from the breach. Another cluster of tendrils rose swiftly like oversized worms, spilling out from the gaping rent.

Seth was sent flying and landed on the floor next to the far wall. The air was knocked from him, and he struggled to breathe. Sharp pain filled his limbs. The pistol was gone from his hand.

The people were easy prey for both packs of tendrils. They were snatched and impaled, torn apart, then dragged down the hole in the floor. Many were taken, including Private Bright, who was pulled shrieking into the darkness.

A tendril slammed into the wall above Seth, and he scrambled away, straight into a dripping mound of spilled guts. He looked back as the tendril readjusted itself and arrowed towards him.

Seth screamed.

The tendril was less than three yards away when a hail of bullets shredded it, and it flopped uselessly to the floor.

Ichor covered Seth, who gasped and held out his hands in some form of futile resistance. He let out a groan and wiped at his face. He was whimpering to himself as Beckwith pulled him away from the other tendrils.

Lost in a traumatised fugue, Seth saw a tendril inflict a glancing swipe across Hanso's stomach. The sergeant's rifle ran empty. He screamed in agony, pulled out his pistol and unloaded it into the tendril until it retreated. Then he slumped against the wall, and was only saved from the other black appendages when some of the surviving civilians helped him along. There weren't many left.

When Seth saw Andy and Jack still amongst the living, such relief hit him that it almost burst his heart.

Seth rose to his feet as Beckwith slapped in a fresh magazine and fired at the swarming tendrils that still pursued them. He reloaded his pistol, working as quickly as he could, and then fired several shots at them.

Beckwith turned away from the writhing terrors and pulled Seth with him. "The exit is just down this corridor. It has steel doors. We can make it." His voice was almost drowned out by the horrific thrashing and busy scraping of the tendrils.

The survivors - the few of them that remained - ran for the steel door at the end of the corridor.

CHAPTER FIFTY

Beckwith was the last through the doorway as the tendrils grasped towards him. He slammed the door shut and tapped the combination on the keypad to lock it. Then he collapsed on the floor, breathing hard. Seth crouched next to him and put one hand on his shoulder.

The tendrils scraped and scratched at the other side of the door.

Seth stood and regarded the survivors around him. Torchlight stung his eyes. Terrified, pale faces wherever he looked. On the far side of the room, a metal ladder led upwards. Their escape route.

"We're all that's left," he said. Seventeen survivors.

Hanso stood against the far wall, leaning into it with one hand over his stomach. He'd lost a lot of blood already and his skin was bone-white. With some effort, he managed to speak.

"The door won't hold for long. You have to go."

"You're coming with us," Seth said. "We're not leaving you here."

A heavy weight slammed against the other side of the door.

Hanso looked past Seth, towards Beckwith, who stood now, reloading his rifle. "You know what to do, Private."

Beckwith hesitated, a quiver in his lower lip. "Y-yes,

Sarge. I know what to do." He turned to the gathered civilians. "Let's go, people. Time to get the fuck outta here."

Compliant and beyond terror and exhaustion, the civilians made little noise.

Seth stared at Hanso, stepping towards him. "You don't have to stay here. We can treat your wound."

Hanso gave a wry smile before his face creased into a wince. He shook his head weakly. "Doc's gone. I won't survive up top. Wouldn't last five minutes. You know that."

Seth's voice failed in his throat. He had no words. And, yes, he knew Hanso was right.

The door shook again with another impact. More scraping as the tendrils tried to work their way inside the room.

Hanso, with some effort, took two grenades from his belt. He spat. He held up the grenades. "I'll give them a surprise. Don't worry."

Another impact shuddered against the door. Distant sounds of devastation as the bunker began to fall apart. There was constant pounding on the door now, the tendrils impatient to be let in.

Beckwith went to Hanso and they exchanged some brief words. Beckwith slapped Hanso's shoulder. The understanding of soldiers.

"Let's go," the private said, all business now, taking charge. He began to climb the ladder. The civilians followed, their panic barely restrained. Ruby put Jack inside a rucksack so just his head remained visible, and put the rucksack over Andy's shoulders. Jack wasn't happy about it, but he didn't have any choice. Andy took him up the ladder.

The door rattled, warping at the top where it had been hit. It would only hold for a minute or so.

Seth was the last civilian.

"Goodbye, Seth," said Hanso. "Don't let this all be in vain."

"I'll do what I can," Seth replied. His eyes held Hanso's for a moment and understanding passed between them.

"Good lad. Now, go."

"Goodbye, Sergeant."

*

Seth climbed the ladder and emerged topside into the wailing wind and sweeping snow. He closed the latch behind him. The others were already heading towards the woods to the east.

He turned and saw the towering silhouette of the God in the frozen fog. It was too preoccupied with the ruined bunker to notice the frail humans escaping under its nose. The writhing mountain did not see all. It was no god, just another fucking monster.

He barely heard the detonation of Hanso's grenades below as he turned away and fled for the barren woods.

EPILOGUE

The survivors hid in the woods with their bags and packs, huddled together for warmth. They waited, motionless like fawns, watching the God of the Wasteland consume the bunker and all within it. Most people were silent. Some muttered prayers.

Ruby cradled and comforted Jack, while Andy stood with his arm around them. Seth looked at the three of them and couldn't help but feel some faint hope.

There had to be hope.

"We'll head north," Beckwith said. "I know of some military bases on the way. We've got enough supplies for a few days. Maybe we'll get lucky."

Seth stepped away from the group. Tears thickened in his eyes as he looked at his companions, there at the end of the world. He spoke with a tone of resignation in his voice.

"I'm staying here."

Andy turned towards Seth, a look of utter incomprehension on his face. "What are you talking about? We're not leaving you here, mate."

"We've lost enough people," said Ruby, holding Jack tightly. "You can't do this."

"This will give everyone a chance to escape," Seth replied. "Otherwise the God will just follow us. It would track us down and kill everyone."

Andy shook his head. "Please don't do this. We need you."

Seth walked to Andy and put his hands on the man's shoulders. Andy looked up at him, blinking away tears. "It has to be done. People have died to save my worthless life. It's time to make their sacrifice mean something. Someone has to survive, Andy. Give Jack and the other children the chance to grow up and make a difference in the future; maybe fight back against the monsters. I've finally realised the reason I survived. I think it's about sacrifice, the greater good. I think we all have to make that choice eventually. Don't let it end here."

"Sacrifice," Andy muttered.

Seth nodded, offered a trembling smile.

Andy hugged him. Ruby joined them.

"You sure about this, Seth?" Beckwith asked.

Seth nodded. "This is the best way."

*

The group was little more than a small herd of prey animals, terrified of the beasts awaiting them. But they were alive, to go on and keep going, to watch and care for each other.

Seth watched them vanish into the falling snow and fog.

"Good luck," he whispered, shaking in the cold, his body falling numb. He'd given his coat to someone else because he wouldn't need it again.

He trudged towards the towering shape of the God, thinking about his parents, his old friends, and all the people he'd ever known. He spoke the names of the dead.

The cold bit at his face. The wind swept snow into his eyes.

He halted no more than one hundred yards from the immense creature as it reared up from the ruin of the bunker and turned towards him. Its huge tendrils filled what remained of the sky. The ground trembled as the God shifted its bulk. Seth gritted his teeth against the flowering pain inside his head, as the God's presence slithered into his mind. Smaller tendrils grabbed him. This was communion. This was the merging of flesh and minds.

Seth's final act was one of sacrifice and fulfilment. He was absorbed in seconds. No more pain and no more guilt.

Full of souls and new flesh, the God of the Wasteland sang its terrible song to the cold.

THE END

THANK YOU FOR READING

Thank you for taking the time to read this book. We sincerely hope that you enjoyed the story and appreciate your letting us try to entertain you. We realise that your time is valuable, and without the continuing support of people such as yourself, we would not be able to do what we do.

As a thank you, we would like to offer you a free ebook from our range, in return for you signing up to our mailing list. We will never share your details with anyone and will only contact you to let you know about new releases.

You can sign up on our website

http://www.horrifictales.co.uk

If you enjoyed this book, then please consider leaving a short review on Amazon, Goodreads or anywhere else that you, as a reader, visit to learn about new books. One of the most important parts about how well a book sells is how many positive reviews it has, so if you can spare a little more of your valuable time to share the experience with others, even if its just a line or two, then we would really appreciate it.

Thanks, and see you next time!

THE HORRIFIC TALES PUBLISHING TEAM

ABOUT THE AUTHOR

Rich Hawkins hails from deep in the West Country, where a childhood of science fiction and horror films set him on the path to writing his own stories. He credits his love of horror and all things weird to his first viewing of John Carpenter's THE THING.

His debut novel THE LAST PLAGUE was nominated for a British Fantasy Award for Best Horror Novel in 2015. The sequel, THE LAST OUTPOST, was released in the autumn of 2015. The final novel in the trilogy, THE LAST SOLDIER, was released in March 2016.

You can find him at:

https://www.facebook.com/rich.hawkins.98

http://richhawkinswriter.co.uk/

https://twitter.com/RichHawkins4

ALSO FROM HORRIFIC TALES PUBLISHING

High Moor by Graeme Reynolds

High Moor 2: Moonstruck by Graeme Reynolds

High Moor 3: Blood Moon by Graeme Reynolds

Of A Feather by Ken Goldman

Whisper by Michael Bray

Echoes by Michael Bray

Voices by Michael Bray

Angel Manor by Chantal Noordeloos

Bottled Abyss by Benjamin Kane Ethridge

Lucky's Girl by William Holloway

The Immortal Body by William Holloway

Wasteland Gods by Jonathan Woodrow

Dead Shift by John Llewellyn Probert

The Grieving Stones by Gary McMahon

The Rot by Paul Kane

Deadside Revolution by Terry Grimwood

Song of the Death God by William Holloway

High Cross by Paul Melhuish

Rage of Cthulhu by Gary Fry

The House of Frozen Screams by Thana Niveau

http://www.horrifictales.co.uk

www.ingramcontent.com/pod-product-compliance
Lightning Source LLC
Chambersburg PA
CBHW030334310726
48979CB00001B/25

* 9 7 8 1 9 1 0 2 8 3 2 4 0 *